PRAYER CHANGES THINGS

PRAYER + THE WORD OF GOD = POWER

BEATRICE B. FEARON

PRAYER CHANGES THINGS
PRAYER + THE WORD OF GOD = POWER

Copyright © 2019 Beatrice B. Fearon.

All rights reserved. No part of this book may be used or reproduced by any means, graphic, electronic, or mechanical, including photocopying, recording, taping or by any information storage retrieval system without the written permission of the author except in the case of brief quotations embodied in critical articles and reviews.

iUniverse books may be ordered through booksellers or by contacting:

iUniverse
1663 Liberty Drive
Bloomington, IN 47403
www.iuniverse.com
1-800-Authors (1-800-288-4677)

Because of the dynamic nature of the Internet, any web addresses or links contained in this book may have changed since publication and may no longer be valid. The views expressed in this work are solely those of the author and do not necessarily reflect the views of the publisher, and the publisher hereby disclaims any responsibility for them.

Any people depicted in stock imagery provided by Getty Images are models, and such images are being used for illustrative purposes only.
Certain stock imagery © Getty Images.

ISBN: 978-1-5320-8051-7 (sc)
ISBN: 978-1-5320-8080-7 (hc)
ISBN: 978-1-5320-8081-4 (e)

Library of Congress Control Number: 2019913529

Print information available on the last page.

iUniverse rev. date: 09/18/2019

CONTENTS

Foreword vii
Acknowledgements ix
Preface xi
Introduction xiii

1. Prayer 1
2. The Bible 5
3. Salvation 9
4. Prayer of Thanksgiving 17
5. Being Thankful 19
6. Praise 23
7. Worship 25
8. Prayer of Repentance 29
9. Forgiveness 35
10. Prayer of Petition 39
11. Corporate Prayer and Prayer of Agreement 43
12. The Coming of the Holy Spirit 47
13. Pentecost 51
14. The Holy Spirit 55
15. The Meaning of Pentecost 61

16. Praying in the Spirit 65
17. All Night Prayer 71
18. Make Prayer a Daily Priority 73
19. The Model Prayer 77
20. The 23rd Psalm 81
21. Things to Consider for a Healthy Prayer Life 87
22. Examples of effective prayers from the Bible: 95
23. Preparing to Pray 97
24. So, let's pray 101

Conclusion 103
Source of Information 105

FOREWORD

Prayer matters to God and through this meaningful writing we learn that **"Prayer Changes Things."** How you pray will determine how you live. And how you live will manifest in the manner in which you pray. God has blessed us all to have direct communication with Him as an expression of our love, an act of worship and to make our requests known to Him. Whenever God blesses something, there is a real enemy who seeks to pervert or destroy it. Thanks to Minister Beatrice, who has accepted the call and picked up the mantle, we are encouraged to fight for our lives, our families, communities, our country and world through an intentional and initiated prayer life.

Minister Beatrice is anointed to help you not only correct what is malfunctioning in your prayer life, but also to help you lay a firm foundation so that you can thrive in your relationships with God and others. Anything that is founded by God will function optimally when it is built upon the Word of God and mixed with faith. Minister Beatrice gives clear biblical references for every principle she expresses. She understands that beyond human wisdom and counsel is the unchanging, irrefutable, incorruptible, living Word of God. When a person gets the revelation of prayer through this incredible book, the realization of the power of prayer begins to manifest daily.

There are some who teach biblical principles but do not live that truth themselves. Minister Beatrice has built her life and, that of her family, through prayer, based off of the Word of God. She is a living example that prayer, according to the will of God, can prosper and fulfill God's purposes. She has written more than just a book; it's a tool, with practicality and application. Using powerful anecdotes, and compelling prose, Minister Beatrice presents a solid case for results through prayer. She also explains the level of commitment that each person must have because she understands **prayer is the key, but faith unlocks the door**. Through this tremendous written work, you will be given the practical steps to make the necessary adjustments in your life. With the correct practice, purpose and pursuit of Gods promises, protection, provision and peace can reign in your life.

As an author of the three books, including the Xulon Press award winning book, "Living to Win," I dedicated a chapter toward prayer as the key in ingredient to winning. For 25 years, my wife, Lynnon, and I have rescued many from discouragement with Jesus being the answer. It has been our chief joy seeing those released from destruction move to victory by using the taught principles of prayer to strengthen their lives. We stand behind everything we've taught on the power of prayer.

We are always excited when we see men and women of God doing their part to help train and build others unselfishly. Their experience may cause them to have a different approach and revelation, but we applaud anyone who is trying to uplift God's people. I am convinced through this book, even the more: **Prayer Changes Things!**

Dr. Christopher Chappell
Grace Community Christian Church
Kennesaw, Georgia

ACKNOWLEDGEMENTS

I would first like to thank God for the anointing under which I was used by Him and His Holy Spirit to write "Prayer Changes Things."

I praise Him for the love, prayers, support and encouragement of my wonderful daughters Melissa Gill and Nichole Alleyne and my grandchildren Kia and Noah Alleyne throughout this journey; to my pastor, Dr. Christopher Chappell and Dr. Rosemarie Taylor for their prayers and spiritual guidance. To my spiritual family at Grace Community Christian Church for your warmth and love towards me.

To Nicole Gill, for her thoroughness and diligence in editing this book, I am eternally grateful.

PREFACE

I was sitting in a meeting day and someone mentioned that many people remain quiet in prayer meetings because they either don't like praying out loud in public or they just don't know how to pray.

The next morning during my devotional time, I felt inspired by the Holy Spirit that I should write a book on prayer. Then I thought, there are so many books already written on prayer by well-known writers. In addition to writing, I had a vision of the book cover.

I began to write the introduction to the book as inspired by the Holy Spirit. Unfortunately for me I was in an automobile accident and it's only by the grace and mercy of God that I am alive today. My car was totaled, and I walked away badly bruised up, but glory be to God for His angels encamping around me and protecting me for I am alive today. I am still here on earth to proclaim God's grace and mercy. Hallelujah!!!

Some years ago, while I was recuperating from surgery, I received a prophecy that I would someday write a book. I began to write my first book but after six chapters, I became discouraged and I dismissed the entire idea.

After my car accident I realized that God spared my life because I have not completed my God-given assignment here on this earth. I have been on various missionary trips to many countries over the years sharing the Gospel of Jesus Christ. I have coordinated and facilitated many revivals and crusades in various cities and have started many prayer groups and prayer seminars in different cities. I have volunteered weekly at various nursing homes for more than 30 years, yet God is saying to me that I have not yet completed my assignment. There is still more work for me to do in His kingdom.

This time, while recuperating from the accident, my daughter brought me to her home where she could be of assistance to me. I would have nothing to do but rest and get well. Praise the Lord! The days at her home with nothing to do were so quiet and peaceful that it gave me the inspiration and motivation I needed to write "Prayer Changes Things."

I trust that by the time you complete reading this book, you will have the necessary tools and discipline for this journey and that you will be inspired by the Holy Spirit of God to pray and be effective in your praying. "…The effectual fervent prayer of a righteous man availeth much."[1]

---

[1] James 5:16 KJV

INTRODUCTION

To your knowledge, has God done anything for you? Yes, well, this is where you start praying.

What is Prayer? Prayer is "Talking to your Heavenly Father, God." Prayer is a sincere inward and outward expression of your heart to a Holy God and creator of all that exists. In other words, praying is the expression of thanking God for all that He has done for you-starting with how He woke you up on this side of eternity one more time; how He has kept you in your right mind and protected you while you slept. It is thanking God for healing your body; for keeping you and your family safe from unseen harm and danger, etc.

Give God praise for what He has done and is doing right now in your life; how He covers you with the blood of His only begotten Son, Jesus Christ.

Satan hates the praise and does all that lays in his power to keep believers from praising God. Satan knows the effect the power of praises of a grateful heart has on preparing one to enter into the presence of God and receive His very best of blessings.

While Satan was in heaven God placed him in charge over the angels relating to the praise and worship toward God. Because of his rebellion against God–wanting to be a god himself — he deceived one-third of the angels to follow him, and God kicked him and his followers out of heaven. Since that occurrence God has not made provision for Satan and his army of unfaithful angels to ever return to heaven, therefore Satan has a vendetta against mankind, God's people. Ironically enough, when man fell from grace in the Garden of Eden, God immediately made provision for his redemption through the sacrificial blood of His only begotten Son, Jesus Christ. God has made provisions for all who choose to serve Him and the promise of eternal life in heaven one day.

Satan is now the captain of an army against God and God's people. He is "The father of lies."[2] Therefore, mankind became a targeted enemy of Satan and his army of unfaithful angels; they hate all those whom God loves and has set out to do all they can to keep God's people from being happy, healthy, prosperous and enjoying all that God has for them.

May I paint you a picture? I hear it said: "when the praises go up the blessings come down." That is so true, only if there is a clear and open heaven.

Please follow me for a moment. God, Satan and the fallen angels are all spirits in the spirit realm. They see what we humans don't or can't see in the spirit except as revealed to us by the Holy Spirit of God. We read in Daniel 10:13 (KJV) that the prince of Persia blocked the answer to Daniel's prayer and kept it from manifesting into the natural realm for twenty-one days. God had to send Michael the Archangel to wage war against the prince of Persia to allow the answer to come through to Daniel.

Praise is one of the most powerful spiritual weapons in the believer's arsenal against Satan and his army of wicked and evil spiritual forces. When we begin to praise God, all evil and negative influences around us begin to dissipate because of the fact Satan and his army can no longer tolerate the beautiful and

---

[2] John 8:44

melodious sounds made by the praises of God's people. Satan knows this better than anyone because he was in charge of all praise and worship in heaven.

As I was praising God one day, I had a vision. I was surrounded by darkness, and as I continued in my praise to God, the darkness began to disappear, and a brilliant light appeared. This bright light took over the place once occupied by the darkness. I began to wonder what had just happened. The Holy Spirit impressed on my heart that there is power in praise to clear the atmosphere and open the heavens making clear the path for our prayers to arrive safely to the throne room of God and for the answers to our prayers to return safely back to us. Hallelujah! Glory be to God!

When preparing to pray, you need to consider what you are praying for and you must be specific. God already knows what we want, but He wants us to ask Him. Then you must get in agreement with His Word for what it is that you are praying for. There are various types of prayers: there is the prayer of thanksgiving, prayer of repentance, prayer of petition, prayer of supplication, corporate prayer, prayer of agreement, praying in the spirit, intercessory prayer, all night prayer, persevering prayer, persistent prayer, effective prayer and fervent prayer. We will discuss each one individually. Prayer is a powerful and effective weapon and the only means through which we communicate with our heavenly Father.

I am greatly thankful to God, first of all for saving me and bringing me out of darkness into His marvelous light. I am also thankful to Him for waking me up every morning and clothing me in my right mind. In addition, I am thankful to Him for giving me two lovely daughters and two aspiring grandchildren, blood sisters and brothers, close friends and spiritual brothers and sisters in the Lord.

PRAYER

What is prayer? Prayer is communicating with God our Heavenly Father and creator. The Old Testament or Hebrew word for prayer is tefillah and it is defined in English as "beseech, implore." The New Testament or Greek word for prayer is proseuche and it is defined in English as: "to wish, pray, properly to exchange wishes." In the Wikipedia Dictionary, it is defined as: "to reach earnestly, beg, entreat." It is "deliberately asking for assistance in a specific area" or an "act that seeks to communicate with an object of worship through deliberate communication."

Prayer is the communication of the human spirit with God. Prayer is simply speaking to God and asking Him for what you want. This communication with God can be audible or silent, it can be private or in public, or it can be formal or informal. Prayer is our direct line of communication with heaven or God who is in heaven. It is the only means by which we speak to God! Prayer is like a person-to-person phone call. We are living in an era of technology; and have available to us all kinds of technical devices such as cellphones, tablets, and computers which allow us to communicate with others in our society today and around the world. These new means of communication allow us to have different types of discussions, regardless of our location and time of day — you could be in the same home, city or even across the globe.

Prayer can seem to be challenging and complicated, but in reality, it is quite simple. Prayer is simply talking to God your loving and caring Father and Creator who longs to hear from us His children through the means of conversation. For some of us it is our hearts desire to pray but we just don't know how, or where to start.

Prayer is not difficult, it is like talking to your best friend, someone whom you know you can trust with your deepest secrets. You know that they have your back and will not expose you to ridicule. God does not ridicule us. He loves us and longs to help us to become the people He created us to be.

It is of the greatest importance that when we come to pray, we empty ourselves of all sin. "Repent ye therefore, and be converted, that your sins may be blotted out, when the times of refreshing shall come from the presence of the Lord."[3] Repent and seek God's forgiveness, then make your request or petition known to Him; thank Him for hearing and answering us. We will talk more about the prayer of petition later. The scripture tells us that when we pray, our prayers must be in faith. "Let him ask in faith, nothing wavering. For he that wavereth is like a wave of the sea driven with the wind and tossed."[4] Our prayers must be in the Name of Jesus Christ of Nazareth. "… whatsoever ye shall ask the Father in my name, he will give it you."[5] We must pray in the Holy Spirit. "… but the Spirit itself maketh intercession for us with groanings which cannot be uttered."[6]

---

[3] Acts 3:19 KJV
[4] James 1:6 KJV
[5] John 16:23 KJV
[6] Romans 8:26 KJV

Prayer is many things, just to name a few:

1) Prayer is communicating with God; talking to Him from our heart. This is the means by which we speak to God, our heavenly Father and creator, of all that is and exists. Communication is defined as: to express oneself effectively. The word express means to make known in words; or to communicate; and effectively is the way in which something acts or influences an object. The capacity or power to achieve the desired result. In this sense prayer, is the ability to come before God and speak what is in your spirit with your God-given power and ability to get the results you desire.
2) Prayer is a discipline. Discipline is described as: a) training expected to produce a specific type or pattern of behavior that produces moral or mental improvement. b) a set of methods or rules as those regulating the practice of a church.
3) The Bible describes prayer as crying out to heaven and pouring out one's soul to the Lord. For example, "I have drunk neither wine nor strong drink, but have poured out my soul before the Lord.[7] drawing near to God[8]; and kneeling before the Father[9]. We get all of our necessary guidance and directions for prayer from the Bible.
4) Prayer is acknowledging God for who He is through the giving of thanks. "Enter into his gates with thanksgiving, and into his courts with praise: be thankful unto him, and bless his name.[10]" We will talk about these in detail later. When we talk about acknowledging God for who He is I would like for you to picture this. Many of you either

---

[7] 1Samuel 1:15 KJV
[8] James 4: KJV
[9] Ephesians 3:14 KJV
[10] Psalm 100:4 KJV

have or know someone with more than one child. There is always a child who is underfoot, telling you how much they love you and how grateful they are. They thank you for little things and for some unexplainable reason that child seems to get more from you than the others. As parents we say we love all our children the same — which may be true — but there is always one who gets more than the others. God loves us all equally. But I strongly believe that those of us who are in His presence and stay there tend to get much more from Him because we are there and He longs to give us things.

5) The disciples ask Jesus to teach them to pray. That tells me prayer can be taught.[11] Jesus teaches them "The Model Prayer," which will be discussed in great detail later. Many of us first learned to pray by reading prayers from various prayer books and reading the Bible. Many of us learned to search the Bible for prayers that are relevant to our specific situations and use them until we develop the skill and confidence in ourselves to allow the Holy Spirit in us to pray through us. There are some consistencies in prayer: acknowledging God for who He is, repenting of our sin, thanking God for all He has done and is doing for us, praising Him for what He will do in the future, and lastly worshiping Him for the awesome, loving, and caring Father that He is.

An effective prayer should have some of the following components or building blocks. They should come before your petition: thanksgiving, praise, forgiveness, adoration /worship, protection, direction, guidance, discernment, provision and lastly petition.

---

[11] Luke 11:1-4 KJV

THE BIBLE

The word "Bible" comes from Latin and Greek words meaning "book." The Bible is "THE BOOK" — a book like no other book ever written and it is in a class all by itself. The Bible is the account of God's actions on the earth and His purpose for creation.

The writing of the Bible took place more than sixteen centuries ago and is the work of more than forty human authors. It is an awesome collection of sixty-six books with very different styles of writing, containing the messages that God desires His people to have.

These messages include books considered the law such as Leviticus and Deuteronomy; historical such as Ezra and Acts; poetry such as the Psalms and Ecclesiastes; and prophecy such as Isaiah, Jeremiah, Ezekiel and Revelation. It contains biographies such as Matthew and John; and epistles or letters to Titus and Hebrews. The compiling of these books provides lots of stories about the lives of good and bad people of that time; about their battles and journeys, as well as stories about the life of Jesus Christ our Messiah and the early church's activities. The Bible comes to us in narratives and dialogues, in proverbs and parables, in songs and allegories, and in history and prophecy.

The accounts in the Bible were not written down as they occurred, but rather they were told over and over again and handed down through the years, before it was completed and written. However, we find many of the same themes throughout the Bible with a unique oneness. The writers of the Bible were from various backgrounds. They were kings, fishermen, priests, government officials, doctors, farmers, shepherds. I am amazed at how God formed an incredible unity of His Word from these various people. He forms this incredible unity, intertwined with common themes and woven together throughout the book, "The Bible". This unity of the Bible is due to the fact that it has one author — "God Himself.

The writers of the Bible were holy men and women of God who wrote exactly what God wanted them to write and were led by the Holy Spirit of God. As a result, we have the perfect and Holy Word of God — "The Bible." We see this in 2 Peter 1:21 (KJV): "For the prophecy came not in old time by the will of man: but holy men of God spoke as they were moved by the Holy Ghost."

In addition, the Bible is a guide for living our lives to the fullest; it gives us a road map for the difficult journeys of life ahead. Put another way, the Bible is an anchor for our life. Within it there is a storehouse of wonderful, exciting and animated stories for children and adults as well. Some of these stories we know extremely well. We tell them to our little children and we use them in Sunday School. They include: Noah and the ark Joseph's coat of many colors[12], Daniel in the lion's den[13], Jonah and the whale[14], and parables of Jesus[15]. There are stories in the Bible which place emphasis on the triumphs and failures of ordinary people like you and me. The Bible is our refuge, it is a great book

---

[12] Genesis 37 KJV
[13] Daniel 6 KJV
[14] The Book of Jonah KJV
[15] Matthew 13 KJV

to go to especially in hard times and at our darkest hour. I have heard many people testify that while they were in prison, in pain and/or suffering or even mourning the loss of a loved one, that by turning to the Bible at those particular times they had the strength, comfort and courage they needed in their desperate hour of need. "All scripture is given by inspiration of God, and is profitable for doctrine, for reproof, for correction, for instruction in righteousness.[16]"

The Bible is a storehouse of insight as to who we are, who God is, and who God created us to be. You see, God did not create us to be robots. He created us with a mind and a will of our own to obey or not obey His commandments. The Bible says we are fearfully and wonderfully made[17] by a God who loves us; and has given us a purpose and a destiny in life. The bottom line is that the Bible is a Holy Book of resources for our daily living. In it we find the standards for our conduct, guidelines for knowing right from wrong, and precepts to help us in a troubled and confused world where evil is rampant. This is why Jesus commissioned His disciples — which includes us — to go, preach and teach others what He has taught us to do[18].

---

[16] 2Timothy 3:16 KJV
[17] Psalm 139:14 KJV
[18] Matthew 2:19-20 KJV

SALVATION

"For God so loved the world, that he gave his only begotten Son, that whosoever believeth in him should not perish, but have everlasting life.[19]" This scripture speaks of God's undying love for the world. He so loves the world; He loves me, He loves you, He loves the fishermen, He loves the drug addicts, He loves the lesbians and homosexuals, etc. When the scripture says "that whosoever believeth," it means that if you believe in Jesus Christ and confess him as Lord that you will have salvation or be saved.

According to Webster's II New Riverside University Dictionary, salvation is defined as "deliverance from the power of or penalty of sin." According to Unger's Bible Dictionary, "Salvation is freely offered to all men but it is conditioned upon repentance and faith in Jesus Christ and proceeds from the love of God; and it is based upon the atonement wrought by Jesus Christ." Salvation is simply being converted to a personal relationship with God through faith in Jesus Christ as our Lord.

In John 3:1-8 (KJV), we read of Jesus Christ having a conversation with Nicodemus who was a Pharisee, and a member

---

[19] John 3:16 KJV

of the Sanhedrin Court. The Sanhedrin was the judicial court of justice in Jerusalem; this judicial court consisted of seventy members including high priest, scribes, Pharisees and Sadducees. After Nicodemus's conversion to Christianity he was expelled from his office and Jerusalem[20].

This discussion Nicodemus had with Jesus Christ took place at night for fear of being seen in conversation with Jesus Christ by his colleagues. Nicodemus had seen and heard of the teachings of Jesus Christ and of His miracles. In John 3:3 (KJV), Jesus tells him, "Verily, verily I say unto thee, Except a man be born again, he cannot see the kingdom of God." In John 3:7, he says again, "ye must be born again."

The Bible teaches us that being born again or having salvation comes to those who believe in the virgin birth of Jesus Christ, His death, burial and resurrection. Without Jesus Christ, we are dead in our sins. In Romans 3:23 (KJV) we are told, "For all have sinned and come short of the glory of God." Romans 6:23 (KJV) continues, "For the wages of sin is death; but the gift of God is eternal life through Jesus Christ our Lord."

Without Jesus Christ or salvation, we are condemned to death and under the wrath of God.[21] Salvation is so simple and easy that many people miss it. First, we need to individually recognize that we are lost and separated from God our creator, because of ancestral sin — the sin that our forefathers Adam and Eve committed in the Garden of Eden. We need to repent of this sin.

Second, confess our sin openly before God with our mouth; confess that which we believe in our heart. As it says in Romans 10:9-10 (KJV): "That if thou shalt confess with thy mouth the Lord Jesus, and shalt believe in thine heart that God hath raised him from the dead, thou shalt be saved. For with the heart man believeth unto righteousness; and with the mouth confession is

---

[20] The New Unger's Bible Dictionary
[21] John 3:14-19 KJV

made unto salvation." Then, according to this scripture, we are saved. It is that simple. Open confession of Jesus Christ as Lord is necessary. It is necessary to verbally confess our salvation so that the devil, his demons, our friends and society hear us confess that we now belong to God and Him alone will we now serve. When we by faith trust in Jesus Christ's virgin birth, death, burial and resurrection, salvation becomes our everlasting and eternal end.

Third, accept Jesus Christ as the Lord of our life through our repentance and the work He did for us on the Cross of Calvary by faith; and invite Him into our heart.

As stated in Genesis 1:27 (KJV), God created us in His image and likeness; spiritual as well as physical beings with the purpose of having fellowship and communion with His created beings — us. God knowing that the heart of man is weak and can be easily tempted and persuaded to do wrong things, placed a plan of salvation and redemption for our souls in motion as early as Genesis 3:15 (KJV). He said: "And I will put enmity between thee and the woman, and between thy seed and her seed; it will bruise thy head, and thou shalt bruise his heel."

God desires that everyone would be saved. For example in 1 Timothy 2:4 (KJV) it is written, "Who will have all men to be saved, and to come unto the knowledge of the truth." A similar sentiment is reflected in 2 Peter 3:9 (KJV): "The Lord is not slack concerning his promise, as some men count slackness; but is longsuffering to us-ward, not willing that any should perish, but that all should come to repentance."

God loves His created beings.[22] Only those who obey His Son Jesus Christ will be saved and on the day of judgment, we will all give an account of our lives before Him.

---

[22] John 3:16 KJV

What must we do to be saved? To be saved we must:

1) Believe in Jesus Christ. "For by grace are ye saved through faith; and that not of yourselves: it is the gift of God: not of works, lest any man should boast."[23] "I said therefore unto you, that ye shall die in your sins: for if ye believe not that I am he, ye shall die in your sins."[24]
2) Repent of our sins: "I tell you, Nay: but, except ye repent, ye shall all likewise perish."[25] To repent means to have a change of mind resulting in a change of heart[26]. Repentance is having remorse or being remorseful of sin, and a complete turnaround or complete change of heart regarding sin[27].

People are usually sorry for the bad things they do, or have done, but sorry does not repair the damage. Repentance will put to death sin. To be dead to sin is to be alive in Jesus Christ our Lord.

Confess Jesus Christ as Lord and Savior of your life.[28] Once you are born again or have received salvation, the next step is to be baptized in water. Water baptism is an outward sign of an inward repentance. Water does not save you, but it identifies to your family, friends and society your inward commitment to serve the Lord Jesus Christ and Him only.

Water baptism is a process of immersion in water which is preceded by repentance of your sins in the name of the Father, of

---

[23] Ephesians 2:89 KJV
[24] John 8:24 KJV
[25] Luke 13:3 KJV
[26] 2 Corinthians 7:10 KJV
[27] Matthew Henry's Commentary in One Volume, age 1833
[28] Matthew 10:32-33 KJV

the Son, and of the Holy Spirit[29], for the remission of sins[30], and to wash away all sins.[31] If you are not saved and you get baptized the only thing taking place is that you went into the baptismal pool a dry sinner and came out a wet sinner. There was no change, just a waste of time. There must be a spiritual transformation of the heart before any sin can be forgiven and washed away.

So, are you saved? Are you born again? Are you converted? Are you washed in the blood of the Lamb and Savior Jesus Christ? Have you been water baptized? If yes, that is wonderful. Please proceed to the next chapter. If not, please continue reading.

Today is the day of salvation. "While it is said, Today if ye will hear his voice, harden not your hearts.[32]" Receiving Jesus Christ as Lord and Savior of our lives causes God to restore us into fellowship with Himself, at which time He empowers us to live holy and righteous lives in Him.

Let's take a walk through the book of Acts to see what we can learn about being born again, or this new birth called salvation.

1) -Acts 2:1-47 (KJV): The day of Pentecost is the greatest recorded day of salvation. (We will discuss Pentecost in detail later.) The disciples were assembled in the upper room waiting on the promise. The Holy Spirit of God came upon them and filled them with the spirit of God and they were never the same again. They were empowered to live holy and righteous lives and to preach the gospel of Jesus Christ. The Apostle Peter preached his first sermon about Jesus Christ and Him being crucified. Some three

---

[29] Matthew 28:18-20 KJV
[30] Acts 2:38 KJV
[31] Acts 22:16 KJV
[32] Hebrews 3:15 KJV

thousand people present were converted, saved or born again on that day.

2) Acts 8:4-13 (KJV): After hearing the good news of the gospel of Jesus Christ, many Samaritans believed the Gospel, were converted and were water baptized.

3) Acts 8:26-40 (KJV): The Ethiopian eunuch believed the Gospel of Jesus Christ once the Apostle Phillip explained Jesus Christ to him. He got saved and was water baptized.

4) Acts 9:1-20 (KJV): The Apostle Paul, who at the time was known as Saul, a Pharisee, had an experience with Jesus Christ on the Damascus road; he became blinded by a bright light; and was blind for three days. He had a vision where he recognized Jesus Christ, and they had a conversation as to why he was persecuting the Christians. Saul repented of his ways and transgressions, and was converted, or should I say, he got saved or born again (God forgave his sins). He was water baptized (his sins were washed away) and he followed Jesus Christ. He wrote most of the New Testament under the influence and inspiration of the Holy Spirit of God.

5) Acts 10:31-48 (KJV): Cornelius, a righteous man of God, and his entire household got saved and baptized in water after hearing the good news of Jesus Christ.

6) Acts 16:13-15 (KJV): Lydia, a worshiper of God from the city of Thyatira, heard the words of Paul concerning Jesus Christ. She and her entire household were converted and baptized.

7) Acts 16:25-34 (KJV): The Philippian jailer asked Paul what he must do to be saved. Paul shared the good news of the gospel of Jesus Christ with him and he believed, got saved and water baptized.

8) Acts 18:8 (KJV): Many Corinthians after hearing the gospel of Jesus Christ believed, and were baptized.

As we walked through the book of Acts, repeatedly we saw that every time the good news of Jesus Christ was preached or shared, people believed and were converted, saved or born again and baptized. If you are not saved, let me ask you like the Ethiopian eunuch asked Phillip in Acts 8:26-40 (KJV) —what hinders me to be baptized? I ask you what hinders you to be saved? Would you like to be born of the Spirit of God or be saved? You can right now. If it is your desire to be saved at this time, very simply say this prayer from your heart believing that God hears you and will do as He has promised. He will save you right now, right where you are, and you will be born again this minute. If this is your heart's desire, say this prayer:

"Most gracious and Eternal Father, I realize now that I am a sinner, lost and separated from you due to the sin of my forefathers Adam and Eve in the Garden of Eden. I repent of all my sins and come to you now, according to your Word in Romans 10:9-10 (KJV): 'That if thou shalt confess with thy mouth the Lord Jesus, and shalt believe in thine heart that God hath raised him from the dead, thou shalt be saved. For with the heart man believeth unto righteousness; and with the mouth confession is made unto salvation.' Thank you Father for saving me. Help me now to learn of you that I may grow in grace and understanding of what is required of me to live a life befitting of my salvation or my new birth. Amen!" Let me be the first to welcome you into the family of Jesus Christ, the family of God — or better said — Christianity.

Your new spiritual life has just begun. You will need to find yourself a Bible-teaching church to sit in and be fed and nourished in the Word of God so that you can grow into a healthy adult Christian. Just as a newborn baby has to be fed and nourished with milk or it will dry up and die, so it is with your new spirit. Babies need a lot of milk and attention or they will shrivel up and die from a lack of nourishment. The same is true of a born-again person. The new spirit at salvation needs the milk of the Word of God. As stated in Romans 8:15 (KJV), "for ye have not received the spirit of bondage again to fear; but ye have received the Spirit of adoption, whereby we cry, Abba, Father." God was our creator at our natural birth; now He is our Father at our spiritual birth. He is a Spirit and now we too are spirit; born of the Spirit of God and saved from the penalties of sin.

PRAYER OF THANKSGIVING

"Enter into his gates with thanksgiving, and into his courts with praise: be thankful unto him, and bless his name.[33]" King David wrote this Psalm. We know David as a shepherd boy on his father's farm in his youth. David said, "enter into his gates with thanksgiving and his court with praise." As I studied this verse, I was reminded of the tabernacle of Moses. It had a gate, a court, a holy place and a most holy place where the arc of the covenant of God was — or put another way — where the presence of God abides.

A prayer of thanksgiving could be broken up into three separate and distinct parts: thanksgiving, praise and worship. Let's look at thanksgiving for a moment. David said "enter his gates with thanksgiving," but what is a gate? A gate is an entrance or opening to an enclosed ground or area such as buildings or cities from the outside.

Gates are mentioned several times in scripture. There are the gate of Sodom[34], gates of prison[35], gates of the temple[36], and

---

[33] Psalm 100:4 KJV
[34] Genesis 19:1 KJV
[35] Acts 12:10 KJV
[36] Acts 3:2, 10 KJV

gates of righteousness[37]. Each of these refers to the temple gates or the gate to the Temple. Today enter his gates with thanksgiving means that we should be thanking God from the gate, or from outside the doors of the church. Scripture tells us that we are the church of Jesus Christ. If that is so, then our mouth is our gate in relationship to the Tabernacle. Don't wait until you get to church to thank and praise God. Being thankful is something that we should do from the time we open our eyes in the morning. We are told "in everything give thanks: for this is the will of God in Christ Jesus concerning you.[38]" Thanksgiving is saying thank you God for all that you have done for me, my household, my friends and my loved ones. This is something that we should never forget to do, always give God thanks for all that He has done and is doing for us. For example: waking us up every morning. God could easily have allowed us to wake up on the other side of eternity many times. Instead, He chose to wake us up on this side of eternity once again, and give us another opportunity to better serve Him and to get ourselves and our lives right before Him. Thank God for allowing us the use of our faculties. When I think of this, I realize there are many people who can't do much of anything for themselves. We are so blessed and fortunate that we sometimes do not recognize all that God does for us. God has given us a heart desiring to love Him and to serve one other, and a spirit that wants to obey His commandments.

Thank God for setting us free, delivering us from our sin, forgiving our trespasses, keeping us safe from dangers seen and unseen and healed from sickness and diseases. Can you think of some other ways to thank God as you enter His gates? David said, "enter his gates with thanksgiving and his court with praise." Out of a heart of thanksgiving, appreciation, gratitude, and praises to God, our spirit is quickened to approach God with the desire of our hearts.

---

[37] Psalm 118:19 KJV
[38] 1 Thessalonians 5:18 KJV

BEING THANKFUL

Being thankful is the result of growing in spiritual wisdom, understanding and in the knowledge of who God is. Living a thankful life is found in those who are in fellowship with Him, their heavenly Father, their sustainer, their source of life which pleases God. Being thankful requires an understanding of knowing why we should be thankful. We should be thankful because "and we know that all things work together for good to them that love God, to them who are the called according to his purpose.[39]" In addition, the scripture encourages us to be thankful for the awesome blessings we receive from God daily, and because of the mighty acts He accomplished through the work of His Son Jesus Christ of Nazareth. Being thankful is an expression of knowing and understanding the Word of God. Learning His words helps us to grow in His grace, love, humility, trust, joy and Christian values. "Study to shew thyself approved unto God, a workman that needeth not to be ashamed, rightly dividing the word of truth.[40]"

---

[39] Romans:28 KJV
[40] 2 Timothy 2:15 KJV

Thankfulness acknowledges that our dependency is solely on God. It comes from our realizing that everything we have or own comes from God, who is sovereign and in control, because He is infinite in wisdom, purpose and grace. God commands it in Scripture. "Enter into his gates with thanksgiving, and into his courts with praise: be thankful unto him, and bless his name.[41]" "In everything give thanks: for this is the will of God in Christ Jesus concerning you.[42]"

Thanklessness is the opposite of thankfulness and it dishonors God and opens the door to pride and dependence on ourselves and others rather than depending on God. This attitude and behavior can be harmful or dangerous to us and those around us.[43] Thanklessness creates bitterness, complaining and a joyless life.[44] Bitterness is the opposite of thankfulness. It causes a person to complain and grumble all the time; never being satisfied with anything. Thanklessness does not see the good in anything and always results in an unthankful and self-centered heart which fails to properly acknowledge God for the awesome person that He is. This lack of thankfulness or gratitude toward God creates loneliness, depression, and a feeling of despair as you tend to focus on the problem rather than on the problem fixer who is the Lord; "Now thanks be unto God, which always causeth us to triumph in Christ.[45]" Scripture admonishes us that prayer should be accompanied by or offered in a context of thanksgiving. "Be careful for nothing; but in everything by prayer and supplication with thanksgiving let your requests be made known unto God.[46]" When we give thanks to God, we turn our eyes from ourselves

---

[41] Psalm 100:4 KJV
[42] 1Thessalonians 5:1 KJV
[43] Romans 1:21 KJV
[44] Hebrews 12:15 KJV
[45] 2 Corinthians 2:14 KJV
[46] Philippians 4:6 KJV

and the problem to the Lord, that we might focus on God and His sovereign grace. It helps us to see life through God's "eyes".

We can begin to see God's purpose, promises and plan for our individual lives. Giving thanks helps us to recognize that God is in control of our lives and is working all things together for our good regardless of how they may appear to us.[47] While all negative situations may not be good for us, God uses these situations for our good. He used the negative and unpleasant situations to shape us into the people He created us to be. He ultimately wants us to be like His Son Jesus Christ, with a heart and spirit of love, of caring and of giving thanks which helps us to keep our eyes on Jesus Christ, while going to God in prayer. "Come unto me, all ye that labor and are heavy laden, and I will give you rest.[48]" "Cast thy burden upon the Lord, and he shall sustain thee: he shall never suffer the righteous to be moved.[49]" It is necessary, as well as important, to live the Word of God. We must not just talk the talk, but we must also walk the walk that we talk. Reading and meditating on scriptures daily will help with our spiritual growth and understanding of God. Doing so means we will have a thankful heart that will help keep us focused on God.

A thankful heart delights in Jesus Christ as Lord, and rejoices in the goodness of the Lord. It also reminds us that we are God's children. "There is one body, and one spirit, even as ye are called in one hope of your calling; one Lord one faith, one baptism.[50]"

Consider these quotes with me:

a) "Feeling gratitude and not expressing it is like wrapping a present and not giving it." William Arthur Ward

---

[47] Romans 8:28 KJV
[48] Matthew 11:28 KJV
[49] Psalm 55:22 KJV
[50] Ephesians 4:4-5 KJV

b) "Be grateful for what you have and stop complaining, it bores everybody else, does you no good, and doesn't solve any problems." Zig Ziglar

When I think of the goodness of Jesus, and all that He has done for me, I can't help but to give God thanks. Hallelujah, Hallelujah, Hallelujah!!! Thank you, Jesus, for your love, mercy, grace, forgiveness, kindness, provision, for your Holy Spirit, your anointing!!! Oh, glory, glory, glory to the Most High and Holy God!!!!

PRAISE

The Bible defines praise as: the expression of approval or admiration for someone or something. It is the intimate relationship of a person or people with God. (The word praise is interchangeable with Tehillah, psalm, Todah, Shabbach or thanksgiving). As we read in Psalm 100:4 (KJV), "enter his gates with thanksgiving, and into his courts with praise." The court, vestibule, soul or mind is the area where we acknowledge God for who He is and for what He has done in our lives. This is called praise. Through our praise, most of us can acknowledge God for how He has kept us alive and walking in good health, how He has blessed and protected us — even when we didn't deserve it or were aware of any danger. Can you think of some other things or areas in your life that you can praise God for?

Our praise is one of the greatest weapons we have in our spiritual arsenal. We praise God in the court of the tabernacle or in our mind. This is the area where we battle with principalities and the power of darkness of this world. "For the weapons of our warfare are not carnal, but mighty through God to the pulling down of strong holds.[51]" The scripture says: "For we wrestle

---

[51] 2 Corinthians 10:4 KJV

not against flesh and blood, but against principalities, against powers, against the rulers of the darkness of this world, against spiritual wickedness in high places.[52]" At times of sickness, death, depression, insecurity, and uncertainty, it is very difficult to turn up our praise. In these difficult times we will need to find the strength to do so or find someone to touch and agree with us through heartfelt sessions of praise to be able to break through the darkness, hovering over us and stealing our health, peace, joy, and happiness. Every verse in Psalm 150 (KJV) speaks about praise. For example it says Praise ye the Lord. Praise him for his mighty acts. Praise him with the trumpet. Praise him with the timbrel. Praise him with the loud sounding cymbals and let everything that has breath praise the Lord. Is that you? Are you an everything that has breath? I know that is me. I am an everything that has breath. I praise God every opportunity I get by clapping my hands, tapping my feet, singing to Him or even dancing before Him no matter where I am. Like the Apostle Paul, "For I am not ashamed of the gospel of Christ: for it is the power of God unto salvation to everyone that believeth; to the Jew first, and also to the Greek. Luke 19:40 (KJV) says in part, "I tell you that, if these should hold their peace, the stones would immediately cry out." I refuse to let any stone cry out to God because of my lack of praise to Him.

I shared my vision on the effect praise has on our prayers in the introduction. As I said, our praise clears the atmosphere allowing us clear entry into the presence of God where we can make our petitions at His throne and have our answers to the petitions returned to us uninterrupted. The answer to Daniel's prayer was intercepted by the prince of Persia for 21 days.[53]

---

[52] Ephesians 6:12 KJV
[53] Daniel 10 KJV

WORSHIP

Worship is defined as: "the act of paying honor to a deity: religious reverence and homage.[54]" and "reverence offered a divine being or supernatural power.[55]" Worship is a humble devotion. In the Old Testament or Hebrew, worship is used in Psalm 95:6 (KJV), "O come, let us worship and bow down," meaning as a way to pay homage to royalty or God. It also means to bow down, to crouch, to lay flat, be humble. In the New Testament or Greek, worship means to prostrate oneself in homage, crouch, reverence, adore.

Both in Hebrew and Greek the word worship means to give homage to God.; and homage is defined by Webster's II New Riverside Dictionary as "special honor or respect shown or expressed publicly.[56]" Worship involves immersing oneself in the act of giving thanks, praise and reverence to our faithful and Eternal Father, God. True worship comes from the heart of one who has been redeemed; washed in the sacrificial blood of the slain Lamb, Jesus Christ. "In thy presence there is fulness of

---

[54] The New Unger's Bible Dictionary
[55] Merriam-Webster Dictionary
[56] Webster's II New Riverside Dictionary

joy; at thy right hand there are pleasures for evermore.[57]" When worship took place in the tabernacle, it took place in the Most Holy Place. "What? Know ye not that your body is the temple of the Holy Ghost, which is in you, which ye have of God, and ye are not your own?[58]"

When we come to worship God, it should be from a state of a willing and grateful heart. In both Old and New Testaments, the Bible shows worship as an act of waving or clapping of hands, singing and dancing. Worship involves some sort of movement. So, how then should we worship the Lord our God?

Let's look at a few scriptures to see what we could learn about worshiping God.

1) "I beseech you therefore, brethren, by the mercies of God, that ye present your bodies a living sacrifice, holy acceptable unto God, which is your reasonable service.[59]" To worship God, we must be a living sacrifice.
2) "Create in me a clean heart, O God; and renew a right spirit within me.[60]" We need a clean heart and a right spirit to worship God.
3) "That if thou shalt confess with thy mouth the Lord Jesus, and shalt believe in thine heart that God raised him from the dead, thou shalt be saved. For with the heart man believeth unto righteousness; and with the mouth confession is made unto salvation.[61]" Lip service is not enough; worship must come from our heart. God sees our heart.

---

[57] Psalm 16:11 KJV
[58] 1 Corinthians 6:19 KJV
[59] Romans 12:1 KJV
[60] Psalm 51:10 KJV
[61] Romans 10:9-10 KJV

Worship from your heart is a time to love on God and to tell Him how great, wonderful, adorable, kind, loving and merciful He is and has been to you. Can you think of some others to tell Him? In your worship time tell Him that He is God Almighty, the Omnipotent One, He is the Omnipresent and the Immutable One, He is mighty and creator of all things, Holy and awesome in all His ways, how much you love Him because He first loved you. You are happy and honored to be His child. Like a child loves on a parent when they want something from them and makes promises, sometimes knowing full well that they can't keep it. The difference is that with God, our Heavenly Father we must be honest and sincere. Remember He sees our heart and He already knows what's in it. Be sure never to make promises to God that you might or know that you cannot keep. God is a God of His Word. He says: "Heaven and earth shall pass away, but my words will never pass away.[62]" God never goes back on His Word or goes against His Word.

4) "Serve the Lord with gladness: come before his presence with singing.[63]" Worship always takes place in the presence of the Lord; and it is not a secret or silent act. Worship involves some sort of movement as we will soon see.

5) "O come, let us worship and bow down: let us kneel before the Lord our maker.[64]"

6) "Thus will I bless thee while I live: I will lift up my hands in thy name.[65]"

7) "My lips shall utter praise, when thou hast taught me thy statutes. My tongue shall speak of thy word: for all thy commandments are righteousness.[66]"

---

[62] Matthew 24:35 KJV
[63] Psalm 100:2 KJV
[64] Psalm 95:6 KJV
[65] Psalm 63:4 KJV
[66] Psalm 119:171-172 KJV

We learned so far that to worship God requires action on our part. We must be a living sacrifice, we must have a clean heart, we must be happy and glad. Lip service is not worship. We must come into His presence with singing, bow down before Him, lift up our hands, our lips must utter praises, our tongue shall speak. There is much to do when we worship God. Worship cannot be silent. "O give thanks unto the Lord; for he is good: for his mercy endureth forever.[67]" Hallelujah!!!

God you have been so good to me in so many ways. May I always give you thanksgiving, praise and worship with a thankful and grateful heart! "Enter into his gates with thanksgiving, and into his courts with praise: be thankful unto him and bless his name.[68]"

---

[67] Psalm 136:1 KJV
[68] Psalm 100:4 KJV

PRAYER OF REPENTANCE

Repentance is having a sense of remorse over one's sins. It is recognizing that one's sins dishonor God, and at the same time it keeps one separated from the one who created him in His own image and likeness. Repentance also is having a willingness of heart to turn away from sin and turn to God in spite of everything. Turning away from sin, and the things that are offensive to God will bring us to a place closer to our loving and caring Father. To repent one must be truthful and sincere with oneself both in heart, soul and mind.

Repentance for some people can be a hollow or profound experience. Cain's repentance after he killed his brother Abel could be described as hollow repentance Cain was simply afraid of the punishment he was going to receive from God for what he had done to his brother.[69] For people who truly recognize what a great price Jesus Christ paid for our salvation by allowing himself to be sacrificed on the cross at Calvary to regain the fellowship mankind once had with the Father, repentance can at times be a profound experience. For some people repentance is reaching a place in life where you recognize that you are lost and separated

---

[69] Genesis 4:1-16 KJV

from the one who loves and created you, God. You acknowledge that the blood that Jesus Christ shed at Calvary washes away your sin and makes you clean and spotless before God, as was the case of Saul who we know as Paul when he converted to Christianity.[70]

God has been calling His people to repentance for centuries "... O house of Israel, every one according to his ways, saith the Lord God. Repent, and turn yourselves from all your transgressions; so iniquity shall not be your ruin.[71]" John the Baptist preached it: "Repent ye: for the kingdom of heaven is at hand.[72]" Jesus called the people to repentance "saying, The time is fulfilled, and the kingdom of God is at hand: repent ye, and believe the gospel.[73]"

It was fifty days after Jesus' resurrection. The day of Pentecost came, and the disciples continued to call sinners to repentance: "Repent ye therefore, and be converted, that your sins may be blotted out.[74]" Repentance draws people to the New Birth, salvation, conversion or to the born-again experience. They are all the same meaning.

In a previous chapter I mentioned that thanksgiving was offered at the gate of the tabernacle and that praise was offered in the court. Repentance also takes place in the court of the tabernacle. The brazen altar where sacrifices were offered to God was inside the court of the tabernacle. Also located in the court was a brazen laver where the priest would wash before entering the Holy Place. The priest had to be washed and clean himself before he could go into the presence of the Most High God.[75]

We too must be washed and cleansed before we can enter into the presence of God. We must be washed in the blood of Jesus Christ which was shed at Calvary for the remission of our sin.

---

[70] Acts 9:1-9 KJV
[71] Ezekiel 18:30 KJV
[72] Matthew 3:2 KJV
[73] Mark 1:15 KJV
[74] Acts 3:19 KJV
[75] Exodus 30:18-21 KJV

Jesus Christ's blood makes us clean and spotless in the presence of our Holy God and Father.

Looking at the 51 Psalm we find that it is a psalm of confession and a prayer of repentance. This psalm was written after David was confronted by the prophet Nathan who disclosed his sin of adultery and murder[76] he pleads to God for mercy, forgiveness and restoration.

Psalm 51

1-2 Have mercy upon me, O God, according to thy loving kindness: according unto the multitude of thy tender mercies blot out my transgressions. Wash me thoroughly from mine iniquity and cleanse me from my sin". His plea for mercy is based on God's grace, loving kindness and compassion for His people.

3 For I acknowledge my transgressions: and my sin is ever before me. The assurance of forgiveness and restoration of God does not come easy. A person who has experienced the joy of salvation and have fallen into the depths of immorality may experience a time of spiritual struggle before once again receiving God's pardon and restoration.

4 Against thee, thee only, have I sinned, and done this evil in thy sight: that thou mightest be justified when thou speakest, and be clear when thou judgest. David is here confessing that not only did he sin against others, but also, he sinned against God and His Word.

5 Behold, I was shapen in iniquity; and in sin did my mother conceive me. He cast blame on the fact that we all have a nature to sin because of our forefather Adam and Eve did in the Garden of Eden. It is a humanly

---

[76] 2 Sam 12:1-13 KJV

natural response to point the finger; or blame someone else for our own wrong doings.

6 – 9 Behold, thou desirest truth in the inward parts: and in the hidden part thou shalt make me to know wisdom. Purge me with hyssop, and I shall be clean: wash me, and I shall be whiter than snow. Make me to hear joy and gladness; that the bones which thou hast broken may rejoice. Hide thy face from my sins and blot out all mine iniquities. David acknowledges that the God he serves is a God of truth and only truth will He accept

10 Create in me a clean heart, O God; and renew a right spirit within me. Everyone who believes in Jesus Christ need the Spirit of God to create in them a spirit that hates sin and iniquity and loves righteousness. 1 John 9 KJV "If we confess our sins, he is faithful and just to forgive us our sins, and to cleanse us from all unrighteousness."

11 Cast me not away from thy presence; and take not thy holy spirit from me.-He recognizes that if God should remove His spirit from him, he will be lost and without hope of ever being restored.

12 Restore unto me the joy of thy salvation; and uphold me with thy free spirit. God restored David's joy; but we see in Galatians 6:7-8 NKJV "Do not be deceived, God is not mocked; for whatever a man sows, that he will also reap. For he who sows to his flesh will of the flesh reap corruption, but he who sows to the Spirit will of the Spirit reap everlasting life."

13 Then will I teach transgressors thy ways; and sinners shall be converted unto thee. You can't give what you don't have. Now that he is restored, he is ready to live righteously according to the Word and Will of God.

In Psalm 51 we see the following components to an effective prayer: A cry for God's mercy, Acknowledgement of sin, forgiveness, God's sovereignty, cleansing, restoration and redemption.

There are several components to an effective prayer. Remembering that God is sovereign and holy we cannot come to Him in any old way; we must prepare ourselves to approach a holy God and Father. We cannot come to Him in our sinful state but must first be cleansed and forgiven. In the Old Testament before the priest could come into the presence of God in the Tabernacle he had to do several things: enter the gates with thanksgiving, (Psalm 100:4a KJV) his courts with praise 100:4b; he had to make a sacrifice deal with his sin at the Brazen Altar in the Tabernacle; today we are called to be a living sacrifice "I beseech you therefore, brethren, by the mercies of God, that ye present your bodies a living sacrifice, holy, acceptable unto God, which is your reasonable service. In Romans 12:1a KJV the priest had to be cleansed at the brazen Laver, the priest had to wash and be cleansed before he could enter the most Holy Place where the presence of God was. This is the place of worship and adoration; this is where you love on God without inhibitions nor asking Him for anything. After loving on Him you may make your petitions known to Him. He already knows what you want but He likes for you to ask of Him.

We cannot give to others what we do not have. We must first be converted before we can encourage others to repent and be converted. "first cast out the beam out of thine own eye; and then shalt thou see clearly to cast out the mote out of thy brother's eye.[77]" This prayer of David is relevant to us today. We can personalize it to our own situation while seeking God for forgiveness of our own sins.

You could pray something like this: O, Spirit of the Living God, great and merciful Father, loving, gracious and kind; awesome in mercy and grace. I acknowledge all of my sins which

---

[77] Matthew 7:5 KJV

I have committed against thee; in thought, word and deed; in body and in spirit as well. I am deeply sorry that I have offended you Father; I sincerely repent of my sins and wrongdoings; and I humbly pray to you, O Lord. Have mercy on me and forgive me all my transgressions and iniquities. With the help of your Holy Spirit, your grace and mercy, I promise that I will change my way of life, and sin no more. I promise to walk in the way of righteousness and offer praise and glory to your Holy Name. Amen!

FORGIVENESS

The Bible defines forgiveness as pardoning the offender or letting it go as when a person does not demand payment for a debt. In the parable of the unmerciful, unforgiving, ungrateful servant, Jesus equated forgiveness with canceling a debt.[78]

Forgiveness is an intentional and voluntary process by which a victim undergoes a change in feelings and attitude regarding an offense; he lets go of all bitterness and negative emotions such as vengefulness, and he has an increased ability to wish the offender well.

Forgiveness starts with God. He first forgave; He has forgiven us much; He has delivered us out of the bondage of sin. Jesus was the perfect example of forgiveness. While on the cross at Calvary, He taught us to forgive. He said, "Father, forgive them; for they know not what they do.[79]" Stephen, one of Jesus's disciples, demonstrated forgiveness while being stoned to death.[80] Most of the time forgiveness is necessary first before a healing can take place.

---

[78] Matthew 18:32-35 KJV
[79] Luke 23:33-34 KJV
[80] Acts 7:59-60 KJV

We will often find ourselves at times in relationships with family, friends, co-workers and neighbors that have the potential to hurt us continually. When we get hurt by people close to us, we tend to pretend that it is alright and that it does not hurt; we brush it off. But the truth of the matter is that deep down inside we are hurt.

Not acknowledging the hurt right away and forgiving the person who hurt us, opens the door to negativity, such as jealousy, anger, revenge and bitterness, to name a few. Jesus Christ taught that we should forgive as often as someone hurts us and asks for our forgiveness.[81]

Living a life of forgiveness is so important in the life of a believer because it allows us to take responsibility for our own actions and ultimately our happiness and prosperity. Choosing to forgive someone is more beneficial to us than the other person. The way we respond to our feelings and emotions determines the outcome of our future life.

Forgiveness helps us to recognize that everyone and everything in our life will work for our good as children of the Most High God. "And we know that all things work together for good to them that love God, to them who are the called according to his purpose.[82]"

Forgiveness helps us not to be the victim of circumstances. It helps to accept people for who they are and not want to change them into who or what we think they should be. Only God has the power to change a heart. Ezekiel 11:19 **(KJV)** reads "I will take the stony heart out of their flesh, and will give them an heart of flesh." Our hearts become like stone when we get angry and calloused by the hurt inflicted on us by others. A heart of flesh is compassionate, kind, loving, caring and can be highly vulnerable at times. A heart of flesh recognizes that though it is hurting it is

---

[81] Matthew 18:21 KJV
[82] Romans 8:28 KJV

possible that the other person is hurting as well for the pain they caused you. I heard some time ago someone said that "hurting people always hurt others" and "misery loves company, because they are miserable they try to make others miserable too."

Placing God in the midst of our situation gives us assurance, hope, peace of mind and compassion in our relationships. However, we must not be naive, but seek the guidance of the Holy Spirit of God to show us ways to protect ourselves from people who seem to make it a habit or a lifestyle of hurting us. As we learn to forgive quickly, we become stronger each time the opportunity presents itself to forgive someone. This is a sign of maturing in the Lord. With Jesus Christ active in our lives, forgiveness becomes a lifestyle.

Forgiveness helps us to see that what goes around comes around. When this happens, we should not rejoice. "Rejoice not when thine enemy falleth, and let not thine heart be glad when he stumbleth.[83]" In a nutshell, forgiveness is letting go of all cares and worries and letting God have His perfect way in our lives.

What an awesome blessing it is to receive God's "free gift of salvation." It removes all traces of fear of eternal loss, condemnation, guilt and shame, freeing us to come into God's presence with thanksgiving, praise and worship in our hearts and on our lips.

The Bible message is very clear. From the very beginning of time, from the book of Genesis through the book of Revelation, God loves us and offers us total and complete forgiveness of our sins, deliverance from the guilt and shame of it and a host of blessings galore to those who obey His Word, precepts and commandments.

In the previous chapter I mentioned that Psalm 51 (KJV), is a great prayer of forgiveness and that we could personalize it to our specific situation when seeking God for repentance and forgiveness of our sins and transgressions.

---

[83] Proverbs 24:17 KJV

PRAYER OF PETITION

What is petition? Petition is defined as: a solemn entreaty or request to a superior authority.[84] to make a request or to ask for something. A prayer of petition is a prayer that includes personal needs as well as needs of others. It is also known as prayer of supplication for oneself and prayer of intercession for others.

"Ye ask, and receive not, because ye ask amiss, that ye may consume it upon your lust.[85]" There are three separate messages in this verse. Let us look at it in three parts. Ye ask and receive not, Ye ask amiss and that ye may consume it upon your lust.

1) Ye, ask and receive not. Could it be that when you prayed that God did not hear you? Scripture says: "For everyone that asketh receiveth.[86]" Could it be that you are asking while you are in your flesh or in sin? "That no flesh should glory in his presence:[87]" The flesh is sinful therefore it is necessary that we get our heart right before we come

---

[84] Webster's II New Riverside University Dictionary
[85] James 4:3 KJV
[86] Matthew 7:8 KJV
[87] 1 Corinthians 1:29 KJV

into the presence of God. This is done through sincere repentance. Could it be that the answer to your prayers are being blocked by the enemy of your soul (Satan and his demons)? Daniel 10 gives an excellent account of Daniel, a righteous man of God. He intercedes before God for his people the children of Israel. Scripture tells us that God immediately answered Daniel's prayer, but the prince of Persia (Satan) blocked the answer for 21 days at which time God sent Michael the Archangel to bring forth the answer to Daniel.

2) Repentance and forgiveness as we said before, allow us to be washed in the blood of Jesus Christ which washes away sin and prepares us to come clean before the Holy and righteous God.

3) Ye ask amiss. The word amiss is defined as: out of place or proper order and in a wrong or imperfect way.[88] This leads me to understand then, that there is a proper and perfect way to make my petition to a Holy God. I strongly believe that we are to take note that God will not listen to our prayers if we come to Him with sin in our heart or a heart filled with pride and selfish desires. God accepts the prayers of the righteous and prayers of those who call upon Him in truth,[89] and the prayers of those who "ask any thing according to His will.[90]" God reiterates throughout scripture: "If ye shall ask any thing in my name, I will do it,[91]" and "ask and it shall be given you; seek, and you shall find; knock, and it shall be opened unto you.[92]" In other words pray, pray, pray. Keep asking, keep seeking and keep knocking. Don't give up or give in.

---

[88] Webster's II New Riverside University Dictionary
[89] Psalm 145:18 KJV
[90] 1 John 5:14 KJV
[91] John 14:14 KJV
[92] Matthew 7:7 KJV

4) Being in right standing with God gives us confidence that God hears us, and if He hears us, He will answer. Scripture tells us "to come boldly unto the throne of grace, that we may obtain mercy, and find grace in time of need.[93]"

5) That ye may consume it upon your lust. When our prayers are selfish in nature rather than according to the Will of God and His Grace for our lives, they will return to us empty every time. Prayers of selfish, ambitious people, and those desirous of power and riches close the door to God's ears, which does not obligate Him to answer any prayer that will in no way bring Him glory. Praying God's words and praying according to His Will for your life will bring pleasant results every time. "So shall my word be that goeth forth out of my mouth: it shall not return unto me void, but it shall accomplish that which I please, and it shall prosper in the thing whereto I sent it.[94]"

Scripture tells us that God accepts the prayers of the righteous;[95] the prayers of those who call on Him in truth;[96] and the prayers of those who pray according to His will.[97] A prayer of petition is communicating with God and asking Him for personal needs, as well as on behalf of others. Prayer of petition also is known as supplication and intercession. Prayer of supplication in the spirit also is known as spiritual warfare. As Christians we need to understand that we have an enemy who is relentless about keeping us from receiving the blessings that God has for us. He is a spirit being and can only be fought in the realm of the spirit. We cannot fight spirits in our flesh or physically. That is why we

---

[93] Hebrews 4:16 KJV
[94] Isaiah 55:11 KJV
[95] Psalm 34:13-15 KJV
[96] Psalm 145:18 KJV
[97] 1 John 5:14 KJV

need to allow the Holy Spirit to pray through us and engage in spiritual warfare, and rage war against evil spirits and the attacks of the enemy on our behalf.

Prayer of intercession on the other hand is coming to God on behalf of someone else. Exodus 32:10-14 (KJV) gives an account of how Moses interceded for the Israelites and God repented of the thoughts He had toward the children of Israel. We can stand in the gap and intercede before God on behalf of others and believe God for their deliverance, salvation and healing. As the church prayed for Peter while in prison, God delivered him.[98] So, our prayer of petition most times is both prayer of supplication and intercession. "Be careful for nothing; but in everything by prayer and supplication with thanksgiving let your requests be made known unto God.[99]"

---

[98] Acts 12:5-17 KJV
[99] Philippians 4:6 KJV

CORPORATE PRAYER AND PRAYER OF AGREEMENT

"Again I say unto you, That if two of you shall agree on earth as touching any thing that they shall ask, it shall be done for them of my Father which is in heaven.[100]" Corporate prayer is the term used to describe praying together with other people, either in small groups or in larger groups of people. It is an important part of the church's function. From scripture we learn that the early church prayed often together. Acts 2:42 KJV tells us: "and they continued steadfastly in the apostles' doctrine and fellowship, and in breaking of bread, and in prayers."

Corporate prayer can bring encouragement to the members of the group. There may be those in the group who are struggling with various issues, such as health, family problems, different kinds of addictions, trials and temptations. Upholding each other in prayer the Holy Spirit brings encouragement and reassurance of God's promises.

Corporate prayer has the ability to join people together on one accord, harmony, Christian fellowship, and praise. During

---

[100] Matthew 18:19 KJV

corporate prayer all people present are being edified and unified in their faith. People praying together, build love and concern for each other, acknowledging their dependence on God for the common good of each other. Corporate prayer brings people together into worship and intimate communion with God the Father.

As people pray together and allow the Holy Spirit of God to bring conviction to our hearts, the Holy Spirit will draw us to repentance where needed. No prayer is more powerful or important than the other — neither private or corporate. Corporate prayer or prayer of agreement is an avenue that encourages you to keep praying until your breakthrough comes. In private prayer, except if you are strong and committed to prayer, sometimes you give up praying too soon, especially if there is no one to give an account to or anyone to encourage you to press on. Corporate prayer brings people together to pray, such as those who do not know how to pray, do not have a prayer life, or who might not pray on their own.

Picture this: you say you do not know how to pray, and you are sitting in a group for prayer holding hands with others in the group. You have already repented of your sins and ill doings, praised God, loved on Him, told Him how grateful you are for being His child and that He loves and cares for you. You have yielded to the Holy Spirit to use you as He wills. Suddenly you feel your lips moving and you hear your voice, you are saying things that have bypassed your mind, you are really praying. How wonderful, this is not you, but the Holy Spirit is using your vocal cords, your lips to pray through you. How awesome is that?

It is important to understand that just because two or three people are gathered together in Jesus's name, does not give them any magical power or any more power that assures them that God will answer their prayer according to their wishes. God answers prayers according to His Will for our lives, in the name of His son Jesus Christ of Nazareth and according to His Word. Jesus Christ is always present when people pray together, and He is equally present when a believer prays individually. "..... I am with you always, even unto the end of the world.[101]"

Corporate prayer is not about getting a group of people together to pray, but it is about cooperating with God through His Holy Spirit and submitting our wants and desires to His Will for our lives.

The Bible gives us guidance on how to pray. Be it in participation of corporate prayer or privately at home: We are to pray in humility, we are to call on God[102] and be obedient to the voice of the Spirit of God. "If our heart condemn us not, then we have confidence toward God. And whatsoever we ask, we receive of him, because we keep his commandments, and do those things that are pleasing in his sight.[103]"

We are to pray in the confidence of God's word: "Let us therefore come boldly unto the throne of grace, that we may obtain mercy, and find grace to help in time of need.[104]" Scripture warns us in Matthew that "when thou prayest, thou shalt not be as the hypocrites are: for they love to pray standing in the synagogues and in the corners of streets, that they may be seen of men. Verily I say unto you, They have their reward. But thou when thou prayest, enter into thy closet, and when thou hast shut thy door, pray to thy Father which is in secret; and thy Father which seeth in secret shall reward thee openly. But when ye pray, use not vain repetitions, as the heathen do: for they think that they shall be heard for their much speaking. "But when ye pray, use not vain repetitions, as the heathen do: for they think that they shall be heard for their much speaking. Be not yet therefore like unto them: for your Father knoweth what things ye have need of, before ye ask him.[105]"

---

[101] Matthew 28:20 KJV
[102] Psalm 145:18 KJV
[103] 1 John 3:21-22 KJV
[104] Hebrews 4:16 KJV
[105] Matthew 6:7-8 KJV

Vain repetition, the word vain means empty, fruitless or worthless words.[106] Jesus Christ is warning His disciples that empty and useless words do not help their prayers get heard or answered by God, it is just a waste of time and energy. Our Heavenly Father is not concerned with how wordy, flowery or eloquent our words are. He is only concerned with truth in our hearts. God already knows what is in our heart anyway, so when we come to pray privately or corporately, we need to be honest and sincere with ourselves in our prayers. Speak to God as you would normally speak to a friend with the exception of the praise and worship which belongs to God only.

It is important to remember that some people aren't comfortable praying aloud in a group. However, we must encourage everyone present to participate in the prayer by praying silently while others pray out loud. One way to encourage participation is for each person who wishes to write a single request or a simple prayer on a note card so others might pray for them. Members could interject with Hallelujah, praise the Lord, to God be the glory, thank you Jesus and the like as we pray collectively.

---

[106] The New Unger's Bible Dictionary

THE COMING OF THE HOLY SPIRIT

Jesus gave His disciples a new commandment: "A new commandment I give unto you, That ye love one another; as I have loved you, that ye also love one another.[107]" If we would observe and obey this commandment and walk in Jesus's love we would be able to observe all the other commandments given under the law. "And hope maketh not ashamed; because the love of God is shed abroad in our hearts by the Holy Ghost which is given unto us.[108]" If we have the love of Jesus Christ in our heart, we will not do anything that does not bring glory to God such as worship an idol, commit adultery, kill, or steal and the like.

After His resurrection, Jesus showed himself to Mary Magdalene and His disciples. To His disciples who were gathered behind closed doors for fear of the Jews, Jesus said to them "Peace be unto you.[109]" In a conversation with Peter about how much Peter loved the Lord, the Lord implored Peter to "feed my sheep.[110]" If we love Jesus, we too will feed His sheep.

---

[107] John 13:34 KJV
[108] Romans 5:5 KJV
[109] Luke 24:36 KJV
[110] John 21:14-19 KJV

After appearing to the disciples, Jesus commanded them to wait in Jerusalem: "And, behold, I send the promise of my Father upon you: but tarry ye in the city of Jerusalem, until ye be endued with power from on high.[111]" Jesus commissioned the disciples not to leave Jerusalem, but to wait for the gift the Father had promise He would send. He was speaking of the prophecy in Joel 2:28-29 (KJV) "and it shall come to pass afterward, that I will pour out my Spirit upon all flesh; and your sons and your daughters shall prophesy, your old men shall dream dreams, your young men shall see visions: And also upon the servants and upon the handmaids in those days will I pour out my Spirit." Jesus Christ is talking about the Holy Spirit, the third person in the Trinity.

When you receive The Holy Spirit of God, He brings the fruit of the Spirit into our lives. One fruit with nine segments; "love, joy, peace, longsuffering, gentleness, goodness, faith, meekness, temperance.[112]" He also brings gifts for ministry: word of wisdom, word of knowledge, faith, gifts of healing, working of miracles, prophecy, discerning of spirits, diverse kinds of tongues, and interpretation of tongues.[113]

Ye shall receive Power. After John the Baptist, Jesus's cousin, baptized Jesus in the River Jordan, God Himself baptized Jesus in the Holy Spirit. We read in scripture that once Jesus came up out of the water And the Holy Ghost descended in a bodily shape like a dove upon him.[114]" Though Jesus was God in the second person He needed to be baptized in the Holy Spirit to be empowered by God to do His work on this earth. How much more do we need to be baptized in The Holy Spirit today?

In the New Testament the word dunamis refers to power, or ability. It is the root word of our English words dynamite,

---

[111] Luke 24:49 KJV
[112] Galatians 5:22-24 KJV
[113] 1 Corinthians 12:7-10 KJV
[114] Luke 3:21-22 KJV

meaning power[115] "force, miraculous power, or ability[116] It also means influential. Jesus empowers us with the Holy Spirit that we may be highly influential in the Kingdom of God. The main purpose of the baptism in the Holy Spirit is the receiving of the power of God to live a righteous life with the power to be able to effectively witness Jesus Christ in order to win the lost to Him and to teach them to observe all that Jesus Christ commanded.

The Holy Spirit's primary work is to teach, witness and proclaim the saving work of Jesus Christ, His death, burial, and resurrection. The end result of our witnessing is that Jesus Christ may be known, loved, honored, praised and made Lord of God's chosen people throughout the world.

The Promise of the Holy Spirit is God's way of releasing His power into the life of all who believe in His Son. Baptism in the Holy Spirit is a work of the Holy Spirit separate and distinct from His work of regeneration which takes place at salvation. The Baptism in the Holy Spirit is available to all who profess faith in Jesus Christ, have been born again and have received the indwelling of God's Spirit. He opens our eyes, heart and mind to clearly and fully understand the great commission and the Word of God. The fullness of the Holy Spirit with His power makes every believer's witness more effective.

Ye shall be witnesses. The Holy Spirit not only gives us the power to preach Jesus as Lord and Savior, but it causes our witness to be effective because He strengthens and deepens our relationship with God, our Father and creator. He also brings the necessary boldness and power needed in order to accomplish mighty works in the name of Jesus Christ of Nazareth.

Scripture shows us Peter denying Jesus three times, and hiding behind closed doors for fear of his own life. Now, after Pentecost, or the manifestation of the Holy Spirit, all who were

---

[115] Webster's New Riverside University Dictionary
[116] Strong's Exhaustive Concordance of the Bible # 1411 from 1410

in the upper room including Peter were empowered by the Holy Spirit. We read that Peter preached a message of Jesus Christ's saving grace in the power of the Holy Spirit with a sense of anointing and boldness. As a result of this empowerment and boldness, three thousand people were converted to Jesus Christ or to Christianity.[117]

Some of Jesus' last words to His disciples "are relevant for us" today. Jesus told the disciples to "wait for the promise of the Father.[118]" He added, "all power is given unto me in heaven and in earth. Go ye therefore, and teach all nations, baptizing them in the name of the Father, and of the Son, and of the Holy Spirit: Teaching them to observe all things whatsoever I have commanded you: and, lo, I am with you always, even unto the end of the world.[119]" Jesus was clear on what his disciples, and ultimately we, are to do: "Go ye into all the world, and preach the gospel to every creature. He that believeth and is baptized shall be saved; but he that believeth not shall be damned. And these signs shall follow them that believe.[120]"

I gather then that as believers when we receive the promise of the Holy Spirit in its fullness, we are able to better understand the Word of God and pray more effectively. The Holy Spirit becomes our teacher who helps us to live righteous lives, let our light shine bright for Jesus Christ and win lost people to Jesus Christ through the proclamation of the gospel.

---

[117] Acts 2:41 KJV
[118] Acts 1:4 KJV
[119] Matthew 28:18-20 KJV
[120] Mark 16:15-20 KJV

PENTECOST

Pentecost means fiftieth day.[121] This fiftieth day began right after Jesus Christ ascended into heaven. The word Pentecost comes from an expression in Leviticus 23:16 (KJV), where God told the people of Israel to count seven weeks or "fifty days" from the end of Passover to the beginning of the next holy day which was Shavuot in Hebrew. Shavuot was the second greatest feast in Israel's yearly cycle of holy days. It was originally celebrated in Israel as a harvest festival[122]. In time, Shavuot turned into a day to celebrate the giving of the law on Mount Sinai. This day of Shavuot became significant for Christians because, seven weeks or fifty days after the resurrection and ascension of Jesus Christ, during the Jewish celebration of Shavuot, the Holy Spirit was poured out upon the first followers of Jesus Christ, empowering them to live holy and righteous lives for their mission on earth and gathering them together as His church.

Before the Pentecost experience, God's chosen people consisted of Israel, along with a few gentile proselytes. A proselyte is a person who has converted from one religion to another, a stranger

---

[121] Webster's II New Riverside Dictionary
[122] Exodus 23:16 KJV

or a newcomer to Israel.[123] Not everyone in Israel at the time were believers; God only worked His covenant promises through the nation of Israel to form a people for Himself. Through Pentecost, God has formed the body of Jesus Christ, the church, made up of Jews and Gentiles equally.

In Old Testament times, the Holy Spirit empowered and regenerated men to serve God from outside of the body. Back then, God did not indwell all believers. "Cast me not away from thy presence; and take not thy holy spirit from me.[124]" "If ye then, being evil, know how to give good gifts unto your children: how much more shall your heavenly Father give the Holy Spirit to them that ask him?[125]" The Holy Spirit of the Lord came upon the priest, prophets and kings enabling them to speak on behalf of God. On the fiftieth day after the resurrection of Jesus Christ as the disciples and others were assembled behind closed doors in the upper room, the Holy Spirit came in and filled all of them with the Spirit of God and with power from on high. This fulfilled the prophesy: "And it shall come to pass afterward, that I will pour out my spirit upon all flesh; and your sons and your daughters shall prophesy, your old men shall dream dreams, your young men shall see visions: And also upon the servants and upon the handmaids in those days will I pour out my spirit.[126]"

Pentecost was the beginning of the era of the Holy Spirit on earth in the fullness of the power of God which empowered His people from within to live righteous lives and to be effective witnesses to all nations. The meaning of Pentecost is a festival of the Christian Church occurring on the seventh Sunday after Easter, to commemorate the decent of the Holy Ghost upon the disciples.[127]

---

[123] Webster's New Riverside University Dictionary
[124] Psalm 51:11 KJV
[125] Luke 11:13 KJV
[126] Joel 2:28-29 KJV
[127] Webster's II New Riverside University Dictionary

After the Holy Spirit baptized the disciples and all those assembled in the upper room, the people in the area were perplexed because they heard the disciples speak in languages unknown to the disciples, yet understood by them. They were amazed and wanted to know what the meaning of all the commotion was taking place. It was a miracle. This miracle happened so that the disciples as well as us today could be effective witnesses of Jesus Christ in Jerusalem, Judea, Samaria and to the uttermost parts of the world.

The ministry of Jesus Christ, the Son of God, who was God and the second person of the Godhead, depended on the Holy Spirit descending on Him at the time of His baptism by His cousin John the Baptist. The ministry of the disciples would depend on them receiving the same Holy Spirit in the fullness of its power in the same way as Jesus Christ. Jesus breathed on the disciples and told them receive the Holy Spirit.[128] What the disciples experienced on that day was a measure of what was to come. A day was coming when the disciples would be filled with the Spirit of God and the fullness of His power. The Holy Spirit would come and dwell within them permanently. "He that believeth on me, as the scripture hath said, out of his belly shall flow rivers of living water.[129]" Jesus Christ was speaking of the Holy Spirit which all who believe in Him would receive. At that time the Holy Spirit was not yet given, because Jesus had not yet been glorified.

On the Day of Pentecost, the disciples not only were baptized in the Holy Spirit; they were all filled with the Spirit of God. While the baptism of the Spirit is a one-time event, being filled with the Spirit happens repeatedly.[130]

---

[128] John 20:22 KJV
[129] John 7:38 KJV
[130] Acts 4:8; 31; 6:5; 7:55; 9:17; 13:9 KJV

To be filled with the Spirit, we must first empty ourselves by confessing all known and unknown sin, seek God's forgiveness and dying to ourselves meaning being born of the spirit.[131] Yield ourselves fully over to the Lord and depend on Him moment by moment for every need. "Walk in the Spirit, and ye shall not fulfill the lust of the flesh.[132]"

We thank God today and every day for loving us so much that He not only made provision for our redemption through the sacrificial blood of His only begotten son Jesus Christ, but He also thought of us enough that He sent His Spirit to dwell within us to help us to live righteous lives, overcome sin and enjoy daily fellowship with Him. Praise, honor and glory be to our God! I trust that this word on Pentecost has been a blessing to you. It sure blessed me as I studied it.

---

[131] John 3:3-6 KJV
[132] Galatians 5:16 KJV

THE HOLY SPIRIT

Who is the Holy Spirit? The Holy Spirit is the third person in the Godhead. He made His appearance on earth to indwell God's people who were assembled in the upper room waiting on the promise of God. It happened on the day of Pentecost, fifty days, or seven weeks after the resurrection and ascension of Jesus Christ, which happened to fall on the same day that the Jews celebrated Shavuot which was fifty days or seven weeks after the Passover.

According to record, three remarkable things took place on the Day of Pentecost.

First, there was a sound of a violent rushing wind that filled the house. This sound of the wind was a picture of the invisible power of the Holy Spirit of God. The wind, which we cannot visibly see, exerts incredible power like a tornado or hurricane does. The disciples and others heard the noise. It was a sound coming down from heaven. The noise was loud enough that it caused people to gather around to find out what was going on.[133]

God commanded the prophet Ezekiel to prophesy to the winds, and to breathe on a valley of dry bones. When Ezekiel

---
[133] Acts 2:6 KJV

did as commanded by God, the breath of life came into the dry bones and they lived. God explains that He will put His Spirit within His people and they would come to life.[134] Jesus spoke to Nicodemus about the need to be born of the Spirit of God. He explained that, "The wind bloweth where it listeth, and thou heareth the sound thereof, but canst not tell whence it cometh, and whither it goeth: so is every one that is born of the Spirit.[135]" The Holy Spirit, like the wind, is a mighty power, which we cannot see. We can only see its effects; sometimes with great devastation and ruin. Such as with a tornado, or hurricanes. the most powerful effect of the Spirit of God is His imparting spiritual life into us who were dead in our trespasses and sins.

Second, there was the visible sign of tongues of fire resting on each person in the room. Throughout the Bible, fire symbolizes God's holy presence. Moses in the wilderness saw the burning bush which was not consumed, because God Himself was in the burning bush.[136] Later, Israel in the wilderness, after their Exodus from Egypt, was guided and protected by the pillar of fire by night.[137] John the Baptist predicted that Jesus would baptize with the Holy Spirit and with fire.[138]

Fire brings both heat and light. The heat of fire consumes the dross, purifying everything that comes in contact with it. The heat of the fire represents believers, who are to be hot, and never lukewarm in their devotion and relationship to God and to Jesus Christ. "Because thou art lukewarm, and neither cold nor hot, I will spue thee out of my mouth.[139]" The light of the fire is a picture of the illumination that God brings to those who are in spiritual darkness. The fire on the Day of Pentecost appeared in

---

[134] Ezekiel 37:9-14 KJV
[135] John 3:8 KJV
[136] Exodus 3:1-17 KJV
[137] Exodus 13:21-22 KJV
[138] Luke 3:15-18 KJV
[139] Revelation 3:16 KJV

the form of tongues symbolic of the power of God to proclaim His Word, or the Gospel of His Son Jesus Christ which brings salvation to all who believes, and purifies their hearts. Paul later stated that the gospel of Jesus Christ "is the power of God unto salvation to everyone that believeth.[140]"

Third, there was the miracle of speaking in tongues or in foreign languages which the disciples had not previously learned. Throughout the history of the Church, the Holy Spirit of God moved unseen as the wind, to bring revival and restoration where He pleased. The gift of tongues is the ability to speak a foreign language that you have never learned or studied. The disciples were speaking languages which some of the native hearers could understand, but which the disciples had never learned. Many years ago, I met an evangelist from Africa who said that his spiritual language was English. He had never studied English, but he said that when he got filled with the Spirit of God, he started to speak in English. He could only speak English when the Spirit of God gave him the utterance. It was not something that he could do at will. Whenever there is speaking in tongues, there needs to be an interpreter because not everyone present would be able to understand what is being said.

God's purpose at Pentecost was to equip His church with the mighty power of the Holy Spirit so that we would be effective witnesses of Him to all nations, resulting in Him getting all praise, honor and glory that is due His Name. As you think about God's purpose for your life today, ask yourself these questions. Do I focus on God in everything that I do? Do I trust in the Holy Spirit to guide and protect me today? Do I know that the Holy Spirit helps me to fight temptation? Do I lean on the Holy Spirit for strength to accomplish my daily tasks?

Pentecost is a Holy Day in which Christians commemorate the coming of the Holy Spirit on the early followers of Jesus

---

[140] Romans 1:16 KJV

Christ. Before the events of the first Pentecost, which came seven weeks or fifty days after Jesus Christ's resurrection, there were followers of Jesus Christ sharing the gospel prior to Pentecost. From a historical and spiritual point of view, the Church as we know it today was born on that day. Pentecost is the birthday of the church. Before Pentecost, or the birth of the church, there was no significant movement to unify the people that could be called "The Church."

On that first Pentecost, many of those who heard the messages in their own languages were amazed, though others thought the disciples and those with them were merely drunk. Peter, one of the leading disciples of Jesus Christ, who we read about in scripture denied Jesus Christ for fear of his life and hid behind closed doors, came forth and preached his first sermon. He interpreted the events of that morning in light of the prophecy of the Hebrew prophet Joel. In that text, God had promised to pour out His Spirit on all flesh, empowering people from all nations to exercise His divine power. This miracle was a mighty act of God at work in the earth.[141]

Peter went on to explain in his sermon that Jesus Christ had been raised from the dead, seen by many and now sits at the right hand of God His Father, and that God had poured out His Spirit on the people who believed in Him in fulfillment of His promise. The crowd then asked Peter what they should do, Peter encouraged them to repent and surrender their lives to God, and be baptized in the name of Jesus Christ of Nazareth that they may be forgiven of their sins and receive the many gifts of the Holy Spirit.[142] Acts 2:41(KJV) reports that about three thousand people were added to the church on that day, Pentecost. What an awesome response to Peter's first sermon, wouldn't you say?!

---

[141] Joel 2:28-29 KJV
[142] Acts 2 KJV

It was the result of the power of the Holy Spirit of God drawing non-believers unto Himself.

I truly believe that even in our day, God could send His Spirit in astounding and unimaginable ways to empower His people to speak in languages that they do not know but others understand. God is no respecter of persons, He does whatever He pleases, whenever He pleases and as He pleases.

THE MEANING OF PENTECOST

The first Christians were filled with the Holy Spirit almost two thousand years ago on the Jewish holy day of Shavout. Seven weeks after the resurrection of Jesus Christ, the Holy Spirit was poured out on His followers who were in the upper room in Jerusalem. What happened on the day of Pentecost is still happening to Christians throughout the world today, but not necessarily as dramatic as on the day of Pentecost. God pours out His Spirit on everyone who puts their faith and trust in Jesus Christ, His Son, and become His disciples.

As we live and abide in the presence and power of the Spirit of God, the Holy Spirit helps us to confess Jesus Christ as Lord and Savior to the world.[143] It empowers us to serve God with supernatural power[144] and binds us together as the body of Christ.[145] The Holy Spirit helps us in prayer and even intercedes

---

[143] 1 Corinthians 12:3 KJV
[144] 1 Corinthians 12:4-11 KJV
[145] 1 Corinthians 12:12-13 KJV

on our behalf with God the Father.[146] The Holy Spirit guides us[147] and helps us to live like Jesus Christ.[148]

Pentecost offers us the opportunity to confess our failures and to live by the Spirit of God, to ask the Lord's forgiveness of our sins and to fill us afresh with His power as many times or as often as we need to. The celebration of Pentecost is a time to reflect and renew our commitment to live as an essential member of the body of Jesus Christ, using the gifts He has given us to build the church and share the love of Jesus Christ with the world. We will discuss the gifts of the Spirit later.

The experience of Pentecost challenges us to examine our attitudes in regard to repenting of any prejudice and injustice within us, and to open our hearts to all people, especially those who do not share our language, race and culture.

In Peter's first sermon, he cited a portion of the prophecy from Joel 2:28 (KJV) where God said: "and it shall come to pass afterwards, that I will pour out my spirit upon all flesh; and your sons and your daughters shall prophesy, your old men shall dream dreams, your young men shall see visions." Peter later explained that "these men are not drunken, as ye suppose, seeing it is but the third hour of the day. But this is what was spoken by the prophet Joel[149]"

In the Old Testament era, the Spirit of God was poured out exclusively and only on prophets, priests and kings enabling them to speak under the power and anointing of God. In the New Testament era, the Spirit of God is given to all believers in Jesus Christ empowering them to be used by God to minister regardless of their gender, age or social position. This does not mean that every Christian would be gifted for every kind of ministry. It is implied that all believers would be empowered by the Spirit of

---

[146] Romans 8:27 KJV
[147] Galatians 5:25 KJV
[148] Galatians 5:22-23 KJV
[149] Joel 2:28-29 KJV

God. The Church of Jesus Christ would be a place where every single person matters and every member of the body of Jesus Christ contributes to the health and well-being of the church.

The celebration of Pentecost is a time to ask God to fill us afresh with His Spirit, and a time to reflect on things like:

a) Am I serving God through the power of His Spirit or in my own strength?
b) Are the gifts of His Spirit in operation in my life?
c) Am I exercising these gifts in the church and in the world?
d) How often do I refill my car of gas?
e) When was the last time I asked God for a refilling of His Power?

Our spirit is a crucial part of our body and needs our utmost attention in regard to the things of God.

The unknown tongue or language links back to the Old Testament story in Genesis 11:1-9 **(KJV)** when the people were building the Tower of Babel. God saw their unity and determination to execute their plan which would have been successful; but God confused their language so they could no longer understand each other. What the disciples experienced on the day of Pentecost in terms of speaking in tongues was the reverse of what took place at the Tower of Babel where God had confused their language. God now gives His people a language unknown to them with power to be used for God's name and for His glory.

PRAYING IN THE SPIRIT

Praying in the spirit is mentioned at least three times in scripture:

1) "Praying always with all prayer and supplication in the Spirit, and watching thereunto with all perseverance and supplication for all saints.[150]"
2) "What is it then? I will pray with the spirit, and I will pray with the understanding also: I will sing with the spirit, and I will sing with the understanding also.[151]"
3) "But ye, beloved, building up yourselves on your most holy faith, praying in the Holy Ghost.[152]"

Praying in the Spirit is simply praying back God's words to Him. The Greek word proseuche is translated to English as "pray in," has several different meanings. It could mean "by means of," "with the help of," "in the sphere of," and "in connection to.[153]" Praying in the Spirit does not refer to words we are speaking but

---

[150] Ephesians 6:18 KJV
[151] 1 Corinthians 14:15 KJV
[152] Jude 20-25 KJV
[153] https://www.gotquestions.org/praying-Spirit.html

rather it refers to how we are praying. Praying in the Spirit is praying God's word according to the leading of the Spirit of God in prayer. It is praying for things that the Spirit of God leads us to pray for. "Meanwhile, the moment we get tired in the waiting, God's Spirit is right alongside helping us along. If we don't know how or what to pray, it doesn't matter. He does our praying in and for us, making prayer out of our wordless sighs, our aching groans. He knows us far better than we know ourselves, knows our pregnant condition, and keeps us present before God. That's why we can be so sure that every detail in our lives of love for God is worked into something good.[154]"

Praying in the Spirit must be understood as praying in the power of God, by the leading of the Holy Spirit, according to the will of God. This should not be confused with praying in tongues. Praying in tongues edifies the person praying, but their understanding is unfruitful for only God understands what is being said. Praying in tongues is for your personal edification and should be done privately.[155]

God gave us the Holy Spirit to instruct, inspire and illuminate our hearts and minds and to aid us in prayer that our prayers may not be unaided, but aided by the Holy Spirit. Unaided by the Holy Spirit, we are more likely to pray for things contrary to the Will of God and harmful to ourselves. Praying in the Spirit actually means allowing or giving the Holy Spirit full control to pray through us in our God-given heavenly language. This type of prayer is quite penetrating and transforms the atmosphere.

The meaning of the phrase "in the Spirit" as in this text in Ephesians 6:18 (KJV), is literally "in spirit." The Holy Spirit was to be "the Place" of the prayer, in the sense of being the transforming atmosphere of the spirit of the praying believer. True

---

[154] Romans 8:26-27 MSG
[155] 1 Corinthians 14:13-14

prayer is accomplished in the sphere of the Holy Spirit, motivated and empowered by Him.

Praying in the Spirit is the means by which we pray depending on the Will of our Father, God. Effective prayer as "the effective prayers of the righteous" is accomplished, motivated and empowered by the Holy Spirit.

We pray by means of and in dependence on the Holy Spirit's help, the atmosphere in which true believers live.

1) As long as we do not grieve the Holy Spirit, the Holy Spirit is willing and able to guide us in our prayer requests, creating in us the faith to believe for the answer to what we have prayed for.
2) As we learn to live in an atmosphere that is solely dependent on the help of the Holy Spirit, can effectively live day by day and be able to accomplish our God-given purpose and will for our lives.
3) Allowing the Holy Spirit to pray through us gives substance to our prayers causing it to be effective.
4) Praying in the Spirit calls for total surrender of self and/or our flesh and to realize that in our finite power, we are powerless against the enemy. We should first ask God to empty us of ourselves and fill us up with His Holy Spirit and immediately obey the voice of God through diligent daily study, and meditation of His Word. Ephesians 5:18 (KJV) reads: "be filled with the Spirit."

For example, as with our vehicles, we pull up at the gas pump often to re-fuel. There are some of us who try our best to keep our tanks full or away from running on empty. There are others who are always waiting until the needle gets to red nearly running out of gas. My auto mechanic once told me, "never let your car run close to empty." He explained gas has sediments that settle to the bottom of the gas tank, and when gas gets that low it pulls the sediments into the system. That is not good for the efficient functioning of the automobile. This is why I do my best to re-fuel my car by midway or before it gets to a quarter tank. Similarly in the spirit, for effective spiritual function ability we need to re-fill often. Being filled with the spirit is a continuous process.

The Holy Spirit helps us in our prayer life by:

1) He leads us into the presence of God the Father. "For through him we both have access by one Spirit the Father.[156]"
2) He deposits in our hearts a sense of being a child of God and an acceptance that brings confidence and freedom in the presence of God. Galatians 4:6 (KJV) tells us "God hath sent forth the Spirit of his Son into your hearts, crying, Abba, Father."
3) He helps us in the sickness of our bodies, as well as in the infirmities of our soul. Romans 8:26 (KJV) says: "Likewise the Spirit also helpeth our infirmities: for we know not what we should pray for as we ought." We can always depend on the Holy Spirit to help us and guide us into the will of God by illuminating the scripture to us and stimulating our thoughts.
4) He purifies and redirects our desires toward the Will of God, for He alone knows and can interpret God's Will and purpose for our lives. "For what man knoweth the things of a man, save the spirit of man which is in him? even so the things of God knoweth no man, but the spirit of God.[157]"

---

[156] Ephesians 2:18 KJV
[157] 1 Corinthians 2:11 KJV

5) He takes our imperfect prayers, adds to them the incense of the merits of Jesus Christ, and puts them in a form that is acceptable to our heavenly Father. "And another angel came and stood at the altar, having a golden censer; and there was given unto him much incense, that he should offer it with the prayers of all saints upon the golden altar which was before the throne.[158]"
6) He takes our inarticulate groans and infuses the right meaning into them.
7) He lays special burdens of prayer on the believer whose heart is sensitive to His Spirit, and is walking in right fellowship with Him. Such burden can be intolerable sometimes. Such burdens were laid on the prophets of old, they got relief through prolonged and earnest praying at times. The book of Daniel 10:2-3 (KJV) gives an account of a great experience: "In those days I Daniel was mourning for three full weeks. I ate no pleasant bread, neither came flesh nor wine in my mouth, neither did I anoint myself at all, till three weeks were fulfilled. The answer came at the proper time; in God's time. When God lays such prayer-burdens on the hearts of His children, He intends to answer the prayer through their intercessions. He will provide the strength needed to pray through until the answer is manifested.
8) He helps us to prevail in prayer by directly inspiring the Holy Spirit, who causes our petitions to always be according to the divine will and purpose of God; which is certain to be answered. Praying in the Holy Ghost or Holy Spirit is cooperating with the will of God; and such prayers are always, victoriously answered.

---

[158] Revelations 8:3-5 KJV

ALL NIGHT PRAYER

All night prayer is spending a night in the presence of the Lord. It is bringing your flesh under subjection to the Spirit of God; it is depriving your flesh of sleep to spend time in the Word of God and in the awesome presence of His Majesty.

In my study and research of scriptures, I found the following verses of scripture relevant to all night prayer:

1) "And it came to pass in those days, that he went out into a mountain to pray, and continued all night in prayer to God.[159]"
2) "And Jacob was left alone; and there wrestled a man with him until the breaking of the day.[160]"
3) "It repenteth me that I have set up Saul to be king: for he is turned back from following me, and hath not performed my commandments. And it grieved Samuel; and he cried unto the Lord all night.[161]"

---

[159] Luke 6:12 KJV
[160] Genesis 32:24 KJV
[161] 1 Samuel 15:11 KJV

All night prayer is not to stay awake all night praying. Its purpose is to encourage people to spend some quality time with the Lord Jesus Christ in church or private. For people who are busy and always in a hurry, it puts them in a place to slow down, turn off the influences of the world with its chaos and allowing the opportunity to get quiet and be able to focus on hearing from the Lord. All night prayer is a place where you can spend as much time as you need, and pray for as long as is needed or for however long it takes for you to enter into the presence of the Lord. All night prayer gives you ample time to pray for everything you need and for everyone that God puts on your heart to pray for. An effective all night prayer is usually broken up into three or four segments or watches with different ministers leading each watch with intent of keeping members awake throughout the night. It becomes the minister's responsibility to seek the Holy Spirit for inspiration, illumination and the fortitude to keep the people in attendance alert, engaged and inspired.

All night prayer sessions are not a place to come prepared with your pillows and blanket to sleep. If you fall asleep, it is alright because your spirit does not sleep, so your spirit will be fed while you sleep. All night prayer is a sacrifice you make before the Lord, know that "he is a rewarder of them that diligently seek Him.[162]"

---

[162] Hebrews 11:6 KJV

MAKE PRAYER A DAILY PRIORITY

Daily prayer must be a priority of every believer. It must be our way of life, and should come as natural as the air we breathe. A healthy and successful life requires being in the presence of the Lord often and having a close relationship with Him.

Jesus Christ taught His disciples the importance of daily prayer.

1) He said "men ought always to pray, and not to faint.[163]"
2) He taught His disciples to pray saying, "give us this day our daily bread[164]" He prayed daily during all sorts of circumstances which sets an example for us today.
3) Jesus prayed at His baptism. "Now when all the people were baptized, it came to pass, that Jesus also being baptized, and praying, the heaven was opened.[165]"
4) Before choosing His disciples, He prayed all night. "And it came to pass in those days, that he went out into a

---

[163] Luke 18:1 KJV
[164] Matthew 6:11 KJV
[165] Luke 3:21 KJV

mountain to pray, and continued all night in prayer to God.[166]"

5) Jesus Christ prayed during sad times, including at the tomb of His friend Lazarus. And Jesus lifted up His eyes, and said, "Father, I thank thee that thou hast heard me. And I knew that thou hearest me always: but because of the people which stand by I said it, that they may believe that thou hast sent me. And when he thus had spoken, he cried with a loud voice, Lazarus, come forth.[167]"

6) Jesus prayed while in agony. "And being in agony he prayed more earnestly; and his sweat was as it were great drops of blood falling down to the ground.[168]"

7) He prayed during His passion. "And he went a little farther, and fell on his face, and prayed, saying: O my Father, if it be possible, let this cup pass from me: nevertheless not as I will, but as thou wilt.[169]"

8) "And He withdrew himself into the wilderness, and prayed.[170]"

9) He sent the crowds away and "He went up into a mountain apart to pray.[171]"

10) We also read that Jesus Christ rose up very early. "And in the morning, rising up a great while before day, he went out, and departed into a solitary place, and there prayed.[172]"

---

[166] Luke 6:12 KJV
[167] John 11:41 KJV
[168] Luke 22:44 KJV
[169] Matthew 26:39 KJV
[170] Luke 5:16 KJV
[171] Matthew 14:23 KJV
[172] Mark 1:35 KJV

The Bible tells us to pray "always with all prayer and supplication in the Spirit, and watching thereunto with all perseverance and supplication for all saints.[173]"

Scripture also tells us to pray without ceasing[174]" and tells us not to worry about anything, and to thank God for what He has already provided for us.[175]

---

[173] Ephesians 6:18 KJV
[174] 1 Thessalonians 5:17 KJV
[175] Philippians 4:6 KJV

THE MODEL PRAYER

Jesus Christ taught His disciples to pray a very simple daily prayer. You may know it by heart already as The Lord's Prayer, but it is actually the Model Prayer found in Matthew 6:9-15 (KJV). As we say this prayer, and we take time to think about the words written in it, and what each verse means to us, we need to make it personal. When we do so, we will find this prayer will become more meaningful.

1) **"Our father which art in heaven, Hallowed be thy name."** Jesus Christ said this at the beginning of the prayer, showing us that He, Jesus Christ, the Son of God acknowledges that God is our Father. For example, you might want to pray, "God, thank You for loving and caring for me and making me your child, although I did nothing to deserve Your unconditional love."

2) **"Thy kingdom come, Thy will be done in earth as it is in heaven."** This verse is about having God's Will manifested in your life now in this earth, not waiting until you get to heaven to enjoy God's best, but now right here on this earth. Ask God to show you what He wants you to do today; how He can use you to be a blessing to

someone in His kingdom; and to give you the courage and energy you will need for what He asks of you. Also ask Him to show you areas in which you might be doing or going to do something that is not in His plan for your life and to help you change your ways. Thank Him for all the ways and blessings He has provided for you thus far.

3) **"Give us this day our daily bread."** Ask God to provide for you physically, emotionally and financially today. Feel free to ask for other needs you may have as well. Also ask for the needs of those whom the Lord may impress on your heart.

4) **"And forgive us our debts, as we forgive our debtors."** Seek God's forgiveness for those things you know you have done wrong. Ask the Holy Spirit to bring to your remembrance those things or persons that you are not conscious of hurting or that you have offended. Take a moment to mentally and spiritually forgive people who have hurt you. You also may want to pray for God's help in overcoming any and all sin that keeps recurring in your life. Ask God for His forgiveness and to wash and cleanse you in the blood of His sacrificed Son, Jesus Christ. Thank Him for washing and cleansing by the blood and believe by faith in Jesus Christ that you are washed and forgiven by your loving and caring Father, God.

5) **"Lead us not into temptation but deliver us from evil."** After praying for forgiveness, pray for God's Divine protection from the temptations and attacks of evil forces around you. Plead the blood of Jesus Christ over yourself. (**The** devil and demons **cannot** cross the blood.) Pray for yourself, your family, your loved ones and your friends. God always provides a way of escape when temptation comes our way. "There hath no temptation taken you but such as is common to man: but God is faithful, who will not suffer you to be tempted above that ye are able; but

will with the temptation also make a way to escape, that ye may be able to bear it.[176]"

6) **"For Thine is the kingdom and the power and the glory."** Recognize that God is the only one who has the power to answer your prayers, and deliver all that He has promised you. Amen.

Making The Model Prayer personal to you will bring you closer to God, your Heavenly Father, and give you a sense of oneness with Him. So, let's make prayer a daily priority in our lives.

---

[176] 1 Corinthians 10:13 KJV

THE 23RD PSALM

The Lord is my shepherd: As David thought about God, the God of Abraham, Isaac, and Israel; and his personal relationship with the God of heaven, he makes an analogy of a shepherd and his sheep. God being the shepherd and he, David, the sheep.

The Bible makes many mentions of the Lord as a shepherd to His people. The idea began from the beginning where Moses called the Lord "the shepherd, the stone of Israel."[177] Isaiah 40:11 (KJV) tells us that the Lord will feed His flock like a shepherd; He will gather the lambs with His arm. Zechariah 13:7 (KJV) speaks of the Messiah as the shepherd who will be struck, and the sheep scattered.

Jesus Christ speaks of himself as the good shepherd, who gives His life for the sheep. The Lord would call Himself our shepherd. In Israel, as in many ancient societies, a shepherd's work was considered the lowest of all works. If a family needed a shepherd, it was always the youngest son, who would get that assignment as is seen with David.

---

[177] Genesis 49:24 KJV

When David said: The Lord is my shepherd, he speaks of a personal relationship; my shepherd. He is not saying that the Lord is a shepherd to others but to himself, my shepherd. He acknowledges that if the Lord is a shepherd to no one else, he is a shepherd to him. He cares for him and he watches over him.

"I shall not want:" This means that all of his needs are provided for by the Lord, his shepherd. It also means that if we make this prayer personal to ourselves we will then say, "I shall not want" meaning that all I desire is supplied for me by my shepherd and "I have decided not to desire more than what the Lord, my shepherd gives me.

He makes me to lie down in green pastures: This implies that the sheep does not always know what it needs or what is best for it so it needs the help of the shepherd because the shepherd knows the good and healthy places to graze and be well nourished. It's like a child who does not know what is best or what is best to do in certain situations.

He leads me beside the still waters: The shepherd knows better than the sheep when the sheep needs green pastures and when the sheep needs the still waters. The shepherd takes them to places where they can graze and drink water and be refreshed.

He restores my soul: David's soul was restored by the green pastures and still waters. This is a picture of the rescue of a lost person or a straying sheep brought back to the fold. The shepherd restores the soul to its purity that was lost because of sin.

He leads me: It is not necessary for the sheep to know where the green pastures or still waters are. The sheep just need to know the location of the shepherd because the shepherd leads and guides the sheep.

In the paths of righteousness: The shepherd's leadership not only comforts and restores the sheep, but it also guides the sheep into righteousness. After David's reconciliation with God, he surrendered his will to God which allowed God to guide and lead him into holy obedience to God.

For His name sake: The shepherd's name is at stake for it is his responsibility to care for the flock, so he guides them with the utmost attention. Our shepherd, Jesus Christ, displays his glory and grace through us which puts His name at stake.

Yea, though I walk through the valley of the shadow of death: This is the first dark place in this Psalm. David talks about the green pastures, the still waters and the paths of righteousness — all these beautiful places. Although we follow the Lord Jesus Christ as our shepherd, it does not exempt us from experiencing some dry places and hard times such as sickness and disease. Under the shepherd's guidance, the valley of the shadow of death is not our final dwelling place. The valley of the shadow of death can be the place where we can re-group or re-focus on our relationships and responsibilities toward each other and enter into the presence of our God. The presence of the Lord makes going through the valley and the shadow of death tolerable. Because Jesus Christ took the full sting of death for our sins at Calvary, we can find peace, comfort and strength in the valley of the shadow of death.

I will fear no evil: Even in a fearful place as the shadow of death, the presence of the shepherd removes and eliminates all fear of evil.

For You are with me: You are with me reminds us the presence of the shepherd eliminates the fear of evil for His sheep because he is with them. The shepherd is with them: "I will fear no evil."

Your rod and Your staff, they comfort me: The rod and the staff were believed to be one instrument with two functions used by David as shepherd. It was a sturdy walking stick with a curved handle similar to a hook. This stick was used to gently guide and protect the sheep against potential predators.

You prepare a table before me: I want to paint a picture of the lavish table God prepared for David in the presence of his enemies. In the valley of the shadow of death where there are all types of devastating warfare taking place with your enemies, God sets a lavish table for you right in the center of it all. He has you sit down to dine in peace. This is what God does if we let Him fight our battles. He did this for David. Do you understand how reassuring the presence of the shepherd is to you?

In the presence of my enemies: The goodness and care of the shepherd doesn't eliminate the presence of the enemies; it allows you to experience God's goodness and mercy in the midst of them. I once saw on television a soldier on the battlefield prepared for war with his enemies. If he eats at all, it is hurriedly. He grabs something very quick from his backpack and gobbles it down quickly while keeping his eyes on the target. David tells us that in the presence of his enemies, he was able to sit down and enjoy his meal in peace because his shepherd was keeping him protected.

You anoint my head with oil; my cup runs over: Despite the dangers surrounding him in the presence of his enemies, David is able to enjoy the richness and the goodness of the Lord. He remains refreshed by his head being anointed with oil; and his cup being over-filled. He has everything he needs. If God were to fill your cup according to your faith in Him, how would it be with you? Would your cup be over-filled?

Surely goodness and mercy shall follow me all the days of my life: The goodness and mercy God bestowed on David, caused him to live in a faithful expectation of goodness and mercy all the days of his life.

And I will dwell in the house of the Lord forever: Though there was some trying times, this Psalm has a happy ending. David has the assurance that he would enjoy the presence of the Lord forever, both on this earth and in eternity. In the Old Testament, to dine at someone's table created a mutual bond of loyalty which could become a covenant between them. A covenant is defined as an agreement. To be a guest of God and dwell in His house is not just being an acquaintance of His for a day. To dwell in His house is a forever thing; for all eternity.

This poem is appropriate in thinking about Psalm 23: "While I am here on earth, I will be a child at home with my God; the whole world shall be his house to me; and when I ascend into the upper chamber I shall not change my company, nor even change the house; I shall only go to dwell in the upper story of the house of the Lord forever.[178]" Author Unknown

---

[178] https://www.biblestudytools.com/commentaries/treasury-of-david/psalms-23-6.html

THINGS TO CONSIDER FOR A HEALTHY PRAYER LIFE

1) **Surrender to the Holy Spirit:** As you grow in knowledge and understanding of who God is; the Holy Spirit will begin to manifest Himself, and the love of God to you. A sweet and beautiful fellowship between you and God begins to grow and deepens within you to the point that you reach a place in your life where you cannot help but to call on the name of Jesus Christ of Nazareth; the one that went to Calvary's cross for you and for me; and tell Him as the songwriter wrote "I Surrender All." I surrender my heart, I surrender my will, my life, my mind, my thoughts, my ambitions, my dreams, my aspirations, my emotions, my spirit, I give it all to you Jesus Christ. Tell Him, have your way in me and mean it. Once you have surrendered your life to Jesus Christ, your life is no longer yours or about you anymore but, it is all about God and what He wants of you. You are now open to all that God the Father has in store for you.

2) **Pray specifically:** Whenever we come to pray, we should always be specific and deliberate. When asking

for something from God, our prayer request should be specific. Know what it is you want from God, make up your mind. "A double minded man is unstable in all his ways.[179]" Once your mind is made up for what you want, you can then begin to cry out to God through intercession. Don't beat around the bush in prayer; quickly get to the point of what you are praying for. Remember that God already knows what you want and what is in your heart. Be deliberate, say what you mean to say and mean what you say, not only in prayer but in your everyday life — be honest. Ask God for what you need. "My God shall supply all of your need according to his riches in glory by Christ Jesus.[180]"

3) **Always pray from the depths of your heart and not from your intellect:** "Trust in the Lord with all thine heart and lean not to thine own understanding.[181]" Trust goes beyond your understanding, believing though you do not see the results.[182] Prayer from the heart is achieved in your prayer closet alone with God and the Holy Spirit. "Therefore, I say unto you, What things soever ye desire, When ye pray, believe that ye receive them, and ye shall have them." That which you have prayed for now, not at a future date but now, the minute you have asked.[183] All you have to do is wait for the manifestation of it.

4) **Pray with fervor:** First, what is fervent? Fervent is having or exhibiting great emotions or warmth, ardent, very hot.[184] A fervent prayer is one of enthusiasm propelled by clean, empty and open hands; and a clean heart that is hungry

---

[179] James 1:8 KJV
[180] Philippians 4:19 KJV
[181] Proverbs 3:5 KJV
[182] Hebrews 11:1
[183] Mark 11:24 KJV
[184] Webster's II New Riverside University Dictionary

for God. "Blessed are they which do hunger and thirst after righteousness: for they shall be filled.[185]" When God sees your hunger for more of Him, He sends His Holy Spirit to satisfy the hunger by igniting the prayer with His fire. The Holy Spirit ignites the fire within our heart illuminating and giving us direction and instructions. He shows us what to pray for and how to pray, be it one of thanksgiving, forgiveness or of intercession. At times intercession can be spiritual warfare with some periods of travailing. To be quite honest, this is the point where most people pull back. Travailing in prayer is work. At times, it is hard work for long periods of time and because we pull back most times we are not delivered. We wonder at times why a specific prayer was not answered. Some prayers were not answered because we did not complete the task. It is like giving birth to a child; all mothers can bear witness to this. After the pain, the travail and the delivery of the baby, comes a sweet peace of the blessing of a healthy bouncing bundle of joy. You have to work through the pain and the travail before you can have the peace of the bundle of joy. Not pressing on would cause irrevocable damage at times, even the life of the baby.

5) **Our prayers must be persistent:** Have courage, tenacity and persistency. Courage that never fails, the tenacity to not give up no matter what, and pray with persistency that cannot be denied. Jesus told His disciples this parable: "There was in a city a judge, who feared not God, neither regarded man. And there was a widow in that city; and she came unto him, saying, Avenge me of mine adversary. And he would not for a while: but afterward he said within himself, Though I fear not God, nor regard man;

---

[185] Matthew 5:6 KJV

Yet because this widow troubleth me, I will avenge her, lest by her continual coming she weary me.[186]"

6) **Most times we wrestle in Prayer:** "Now I beseech you, brethren, for the Lord Jesus Christ's sake, and for the love of the Spirit, that ye strive together with me in your prayers to God for me,[187]" The word strive in this text comes from the Greek word agonize meaning to wrestle, or fight. Many people say that we are to humbly approach God as little children, quietly trusting Him for what it is that we desire, and believe that we receive it. This is true, but it does not stop there as that is not all there is to prayer. This is just the first part of the petition. Paul puts it this way, "Fight the good fight of faith, lay hold on eternal life, whereunto thou art also called, and hast professed a good profession before many witnesses.[188]" We are to fight the good fight of faith. The devil will have his demons do whatever it takes to keep you from receiving the very best from God, like the answers to your prayers and he will also block as many of your blessings that he can. That is why at times you will have to wrestle with the enemy in the power of the Holy Spirit. "For we wrestle not against flesh and blood, but against principalities, against powers, against the rulers of the darkness of this world, against spiritual wickedness in high places.[189]" The Holy Spirit wins over the devil and his demons every time! Hallelujah!!!

7) **Praise follows Prayer:** As God has answered your prayer and given you the desire of your heart, we should never deny Him the praise that is due His name. Always express your sincere gratitude to God for all that He has and is

---

[186] Luke 18:1-8 KJV
[187] Romans 15:30 KJV
[188] 1 Timothy 6:12 KJV
[189] Ephesians 6:12 KJV

doing for us and our loved ones. Not to give God praise, honor and glory for answered prayer is a sign of ingratitude and ingratitude at some point in life will eventually become quite costly. Praises to God should be heartfelt, deliberate and come from our lips full of fervor "I will bless the Lord at all times: his praise shall continually be in my mouth. My soul shall make her boast in the Lord: the humble shall hear thereof, and be glad. O magnify the Lord with me, and let us exalt his name together.[190]" You see, to bless the Lord brings blessings to others. So, let's share the blessings by praising God that others may hear of it and be blessed. To dance before the Lord is a type of praise. "And David danced before the Lord with all his might.[191]" Dancing, as with any form of exercise, causes the blood to flow rapidly through the veins and make the heart beat at a healthier pace. Dancing is a great exercise, especially done in the presence of the Lord.

8) **Praying for our Pastors:** "Now I beseech you, brethren, for the Lord Jesus Christ's sake, and for the love of the Spirit, that ye strive together with me in your prayers to God for me.[192]" If the Apostle Paul, a chosen vessel of God, stands in need of the prayer and intercession by his Christian members, the ordinary ministers of the Gospel of Jesus Christ, how much more do we need prayer and intercession of the saints "I exhort therefore, that, first of all, supplications, prayers, intercessions, and giving of thanks, be made for all men; For kings, and for all that are in authority; that we may lead a quiet and peaceable life in all godliness and honesty. For this is good and acceptable

---

[190] Psalm 34:1-3 KJV
[191] 2 Samuel 6:14 KJV
[192] Romans 15:30 KJV

in the sight of God our Savior; Who will have all men to be saved, and to come unto the knowledge of the truth.[193]"

9) We pray for our pastors, ministers and leaders out of a heart of love and a sense of gratitude for their service and watchful eye over us and their laboring in the Word of God and His Doctrine to be able to properly share God's word with us to bring us to a place of salvation in God. We pray that they would: "Study to shew thyself approved unto God, a workman that needeth not to be ashamed, rightly dividing the word of truth.[194]" In answer to our heartfelt prayers, God will grant our pastors, ministers, leaders and government officials a double portion of His anointing. They will be empowered for their assignment and for them to be able to operate and function in their daily unforeseen challenges awaiting them on their journey. Pray that our pastors will share God's word and the good news of Jesus Christ; that conviction will fall on those who hear the word and do not yet know the Lord Jesus Christ, that they will be saved.

10) **Effective Prayer:** The word effective is defined as the capacity or power to achieve the desired result.[195] To pray and not get results and answers to our prayers is simply a waste of time. Effective prayer is one requiring true faith and the right relationship with the Lord Jesus Christ. Effective prayer is one that requires true faith and a right relationship with the Lord Jesus Christ. I say this because:

---

[193] 1 Timothy 2:1-4 KJV
[194] 2 Timothy 2:15 KJV
[195] Webster's II New Riverside University Dictionary

a) Jesus Christ says: "Therefore I say unto you, What things soever ye desire, when ye pray, believe that ye receive them, and ye shall have them.[196]"
b) For our prayers to be effective it must be made in the name of Jesus Christ of Nazareth.[197]
c) Our prayers can only be effective if made according to the perfect will of God[198] we must be in God's will.[199]
d) Our prayers must be persistent.[200]
e) Effective prayer must have praise, and adoration in it.[201]

---

[196] Mark 11:24 KJV
[197] John 14:13 KJV
[198] John 5:14 KJV
[199] Matthew 6:33 KJV
[200] Luke 18:1-8 KJV
[201] Psalm 150 KJV

EXAMPLES OF EFFECTIVE PRAYERS FROM THE BIBLE:

Moses: Moses had many answered prayers from God, in particular; "And the Lord said unto Moses, I have seen this people, and, behold, it is a stiff-necked people: Now therefore let me alone, that my wrath may wax hot against them, and that I may consume them: and I will make of thee a great nation. And Moses besought the Lord his God, and said, Lord, why doth thy wrath wax hot against thy people, which thou hast brought forth out of the land of Egypt with great power, and with a mighty hand? Wherefore should the Egyptians speak, and say, For mischief did he bring them out, to slay them in the mountains, and to consume them from the face of the earth? Turn from thy fierce wrath, and repent of this evil against thy people. Remember Abraham, Isaac, and Israel, thy servants, to whom thou swarest by thine own self, and saidst unto them, I will multiply your seed as the stars of heaven, and all this land that I have spoken of will I give unto your seed, and they shall inherit it for ever. And the Lord repented of the evil which he thought to do unto his people.[202]" Effective prayer can change God's mind as we see happened here.

Sampson: Sampson prayed to God for another opportunity to fulfill his life's task of defeating the Philistines, God gave him strength to pull down the pillars of the building in which they were celebrating the power of their gods. This is what he prayed: "O Lord God, remember me, I pray thee, and strengthen me, I pray thee, only this once, O God, that I may be at once avenged of the Philistines for my two eyes.[203]"

Elijah: Also known as Elias in the New Testament. He had many of his prayers answered and he brought glory to the God of Israel. "Elias was a man subject to like passions as we are, and he prayed earnestly that it might not rain: and it rained not on the earth by the space of three years and six months. And he prayed again, and the heaven gave rain, and the earth brought forth her fruit.[204]"

Hezekiah: He was sick and the prophet Isaiah told him that he was going to die. So Hezekiah turned his face to the wall and prayed intensely for God to give him more years to live. God heard his prayer and immediately gave him fifteen more years.[205]

The early Church: While Peter was in prison the church prayed earnestly without ceasing for him and Peter was miraculously released from prison.[206]

---

[202] Exodus 32:7-14 KJV
[203] Judges 16:28 KJV
[204] James 5:17-18 KJV
[205] 2 Kings 20 KJV
[206] Acts 12:3-11 KJV

PREPARING TO PRAY

Remember, "God is a Spirit" and He is Holy. "They that worship him must worship him in spirit and in truth.[207]" The first thing we must remember to do when coming to God in prayer is to come clean before Him; by this I mean have no unforgiven sin in your heart, be sure to repent of all evil and wrongdoing in your heart toward anyone consciously and unconsciously. "If we confess our sins, he is faithful and just to forgive us our sins, and to cleanse us from all unrighteousness.[208]" Find scriptures that are relevant to your situation and pray them back to God. Don't be in a hurry, ask the Holy Spirit to show you areas in you that are not clean and pleasing to God, then yield to Him and allow Him to clean you up. When you are done confessing your sin, ask God to wash you in the sacrificial blood of the Lamb, Jesus Christ.

"For the Word of God is quick, and powerful, and sharper than any twoedged sword, piercing even to the dividing asunder of soul and spirit, and of joints and marrow, and is a discerner of the thoughts and intents of the heart.[209]"

---

[207] John 4:24 KJV
[208] 1 John 1:9 KJV
[209] Hebrews 4:12 KJV

"So shall my word be that goeth forth out of my mouth: it shall not return unto me void, but it shall accomplish that which I please, and it shall prosper in the thing whereto I sent it.[210]"

Let's begin; let's look at the Psalms and see which ones we could use as we pray.

1) "I will bless the Lord at all times: and his praise shall continually be in my mouth.[211]"
2) "O Lord thou hast searched me, and known me. Thou knowest my downsitting and mine uprising, thou understandest my thought afar off. Thou compassest my path and my lying down, and art acquainted with all my ways.[212]"
3) "Deliver me, O Lord, from the evil man: preserve me from the violent man.[213]" The Word of God is extremely powerful and it will do exactly what God says.
4) "Lord I cry unto thee: make haste unto me; give ear unto my voice, when I cry unto thee. Let my prayer be set forth before thee as incense; and the lifting up of my hands as the evening sacrifice. Set a watch O Lord, before my mouth; keep the door of my lips.[214]"
5) "Create in me a heart, O God; and renew a right spirit within me. Cast me not away from thy presence; and take not thy holy spirit from me. Restore unto me the joy of thy salvation; and uphold me with thy free spirit. Then will I teach transgressors thy ways; and sinners shall be converted unto thee. Deliver me from bloodguiltiness, O God, thou God of my salvation: and my tongue shall sing

---

[210] Isaiah 55:11 KJV
[211] Psalm 34:1 KJV
[212] Psalm 139:1-3 KJV
[213] Psalm 140:1 KJV
[214] Psalm 141:1-3 KJV

aloud of thy righteousness.[215]" This Psalm is a great prayer of repentance and forgiveness.

6) "I will praise thee with my whole heart: before the gods will I sing praise unto thee. I will worship toward thy holy temple, and praise thy name for thy lovingkindness and for thy truth: for thou hast magnified thy word above all thy name. ... Thou I walk in the midst of trouble, thou wilt revive me: thou shalt stretch forth thine hand against the wrath of mine enemies, and thy right hand shall save me. The Lord will perfect that which concerneth me: thy mercy, O Lord, endureth for ever: forsake not the works of thine own hands.[216]"

7) "O give thanks unto the Lord; for He is good: for his mercy endureth for ever.[217]"

Love on God for a moment, He has been good and great to you. Thank Him for all that He has done and is doing for you even at this very minute. Praise Him and worship Him for who He is: just awesome, holy, merciful, caring and a loving Father.

---

[215] Psalm 51:10-14 KJV
[216] Psalm 138:1-2; 7-8 KJV
[217] Psalm 136:1 KJV

SO, LET'S PRAY

Spirit of the Living God, I humbly come before you this day seeking your forgiveness of my sins and all unrighteousness, wash me in the precious blood of the sacrificial Lamb, Jesus Christ of Nazareth. Your word declares in 1 John 1:9 (KJV) that if I confess my sins, you are faithful to forgive and cleanse me. Thank you for forgiving and cleansing me of all sin. I thank you Father for my salvation through Jesus Christ Your Son. I praise You for all that you have done for me thus far even when I have not been deserving and I worship you for who you are: loving, caring, forgiving, merciful, almighty, omnipotent and omniscient. I give honor and glory to your name. Help me Lord, to allow the light of Your Holy Spirit to shine through me always, that men will see it and be drawn to you for You will that none shall perish but that all may come to repentance. "The Lord is not slack concerning his promise, as some men count slackness; but is longsuffering to us-ward, not willing that any should perish, but that all should come to repentance.[218]"

Here is where you make your petition. Lord, you said: "Ask, and it shall be given you; seek, and ye shall find; knock, and it

---

[218] 2 Peter 3:9 KJV

shall be opened unto you: For every one that asketh receiveth; and he that seeketh findeth; and to him that knocketh it shall be opened.[219]" (**Include your petition.**) Lord I am asking in faith believing that you have heard me, and I wait in expectation for the answer to my prayer. "But let him ask in faith, nothing wavering. For he that wavereth is like a wave of the sea driven with the wind and tossed.[220]" "So shall my word be that goeth forth out of my mouth: it shall not return unto me void, but it shall accomplish that which I please, and it shall prosper in the thing whereto I sent it.[221]"

Thank God for the answer to your prayers; thou you do not see it yet. Avoid vain repetitions when you pray. "But when ye pray, use not vain repetitions, as the heathen do: for they think that they shall be heard for their much speaking.[222]"

Speak to God as you would speak to a friend. God calls you friend. When you speak to your friend you do not repeatedly call their name every other word you speak, do you? So why pray that way to God? Maybe because you have heard someone pray that way and you have copied it. Be yourself. Let the Holy Spirit teach you how to pray and develop your own prayer style.

Thank you, Father, for loving me, thank You for Your grace and mercy toward me. I love you Lord, get glory out of my life, help me to live for you and gladly accept your call on my life. I pray this prayer in the name of Jesus Christ of Nazareth. Amen! Amen!

Put this prayer in your own words, better yet, let the Holy Spirit of God lead you into prayer and allow Him to pray through you. He knows how and what you should pray for.

---

[219] Matthew 7:7-8 KJV
[220] James 1:6 KJV
[221] Isaiah 55:11 KJV
[222] Matthew 6:7 KJV

CONCLUSION

As I conclude I would like to say that this journey in writing this book, "Prayer Changes Things," has been a delight for me as well as spiritually awakening and rewarding. Not in a million years would I think that though prophesied twice I could write a book — any book — much less one on prayer. I thank God for this opportunity to serve Him in this manner. It truly was a joy and pleasure for me as well as to make the time needed to spend with God and to hear from Him regarding what He wanted me to write in this book, "Prayer Changes Things." It is my heartfelt desire that at this point in your reading, you have been able to free yourself of any and all inhibitions you may have regarding prayer. I also hope that you have gotten deliverance in areas where the enemy of your soul has been lying to you, keeping you bound and confused; telling you that you can't pray, because you do not know how, that you are not worthy, or that you have sin in your life and God will not hear you. Know that that is not true, it is a lie from the father of lies.

I have given you tools to be able to successfully accomplish the task of praying. It is a beautiful and rewarding task, believe me. It is one that you will enjoy and wonder why you had not reached here before now. It is also spiritually rewarding to be able to enter into the presence of the Lord without any inhibitions, knowing that He gladly looks forward to your coming and that it delights Him when you come and not rush to leave.

Once you are able to enter into the presence of God through prayer you will never be the same again. You will want more and more of God each and every day. That is a great thing, enjoy the journey, enjoy every moment spent in the presence of your loving heavenly Father. It is a good practice, for one day you will live there forever. I have found that time spent in the presence of the Lord has been peaceful, extremely restful, highly rewarding, abundantly refreshing and powerfully empowering. God Richly Bless you is my prayer! Enjoy the journey!

SOURCE OF INFORMATION

1. King James Bible
2. The Full Life Study Bible
3. Strong's Exhaustive Concordance
4. The New Unger's Bible Dictionary
5. Webster's II New Riverside University Dictionary
6. Mathew Henry Commentary

CPSIA information can be obtained
at www.ICGtesting.com
Printed in the USA
LVHW040056170920
666285LV00002B/366